Epiphany

Epiphany
a novella

PAUL McCUSKER

ZondervanPublishingHouse
Grand Rapids, Michigan

A Division of HarperCollins*Publishers*

Epiphany
Copyright © 1998 by Paul McCusker

Requests for information should be addressed to:

 ZondervanPublishingHouse
Grand Rapids, Michigan 49530

Library of Congress Cataloging-in-Publication Data

McCusker, Paul, 1958–
    Epiphany : one family's Christmas discovery / Paul McCusker.
       p.   cm.
    ISBN: 0-310-22545-0
    I. Title.
  PS3563.C3533E65   1998
  813'.54—dc21
                                                       98-28854
                                                            CIP

All Scripture quotations, unless otherwise indicated, are taken from the *Holy Bible: New International Version*®. NIV®. Copyright © 1973, 1978, 1984 by International Bible Society. Used by permission of Zondervan Publishing House. All rights reserved.

Published in association with the literary agency of Alive Communications, Inc., 1465 Kelly Johnson Blvd., #320, Colorado Springs, CO 80920

Interior design by Sherri L. Hoffman

Cover and interior illustration by Joe Burleson

Printed in the United States of America

98 99 00 01 02 03 04 /❖ DC/ 10 9 8 7 6 5 4 3 2 1

To Dan Miller

for all those Christmases so long ago.

One

I've always been a big fan of being alive. Not a day has gone by that I didn't wake up in the morning and in some way thank God for letting me draw another breath. In both good times and bad, I have believed that life was a gift—a treasure—not to be wasted. All this to say that I've tried to make the most of my days. And I suppose, like most people, I expected to live a long time. Which is why I was surprised and disappointed that I died at the young age of sixty-two.

My name is Richard Lee, by the way.

It was a stupid accident that killed me; one I'm a little embarrassed to confess. I had gone to the pond behind my house. Not directly behind the house, but down the path through the grove of pine trees, just beyond the stone bridge. I loved to walk there first thing in the morning and sometimes in the afternoons. Copper, my Labrador, demanded it up until the day he died. We had our morning and afternoon walks to the pond to observe the gentle ripple of the water, the pebbled shore, the soft earth, and balding patches of grass and weeds.

It was a haven, as familiar to us as our mutual old age. And yet, like age, it was full of just as much mystery. Who knew what we would find there? New ducklings, a species of bug we'd never noticed before, fallen leaves of beautiful color and design, a subtle change in the shape of the pond after a particularly bad rain. The wonder of it all.

Even after I lost Copper I continued the routine to the pond. The pond was changing though—and not always for the better. A developer had bought up Cahill's property to the west of my modest acreage, and cardboard boxes that pretended to be houses had been quickly assembled. They called the development Quail Run, though I've never seen a quail in the area. With the houses, of course, came people. I didn't mind that. I like people. But some of those people had teenagers who'd decided that my pond was a good place to socialize. I don't even mind that—but they had a lack of respect for the pond that bothered me. Coke cans, food wrappers, and cigarette butts threatened to destroy the natural wonder of my haven.

Just this morning—if it *was* this morning, I can't be sure right now—I had bought a Christmas tree from Billy Atkinson's farm, and he and I lugged it into my living room. Then I had pulled boxes of Christmas ornaments down from the attic. My plan was to get everything set up for Christmas, then maybe grab the mail and go down to the Park 'n Dine for a blue-plate special. Those were weaknesses of mine: the mail, the Park 'n Dine, and their blue-plate specials. For me there was magic in all three. The mail because it had letters, magazines, or even the odd manuscript from someone who didn't know I'd retired from my little publishing business.

The Park 'n Dine because it was an old fifties-style diner with red cushions and chrome railings, beveled mirrors behind the pie rack, and classic rock-and-roll on the Wurlitzer jukebox. The blue-plate special because there was a lot of food for not a lot of money.

But I had to have my walk to the pond first. It was a crisp December day; the kind of day that made me feel alive, with the air so frosty it tingled my cheeks and so fresh it felt cleansing to breathe it. The iced puddles on the hard earth cracked beneath my rubber-soled boots as I walked. It had snowed last night, so I was pretty sure the teenagers had stayed inside their homes and left my pond alone. It would be mine again, I was certain.

And it was. The snow had given way to a deeper freeze before dawn, so that the trees wore a magical coat of sparkling icicles. White clung to the world like an old glove. The pond had a layer of ice that skimmed the surface like a sugar glaze. I took my place by the large rock—*my* spot for years—and thought of Copper first, imagining I could hear him padding around, sniffing and barking at unseen intruders.

For a moment I thought of my wife, Kathryn, as a younger woman, gesturing happily at a new discovery she'd made on the edge of the water. She often came down to the pond with me. Later, age was less kind and she developed painful arthritis in her knees and ankles. She reluctantly bequeathed the pond to Copper and me. Our children had grown up and left by then. From my rock this morning, I thought of them, too.

More specifically, I had been thinking of a small boat my second son, Jonathan, had built in his tenth summer.

I remembered it there, bobbing on the water, in danger of capsizing—when suddenly the memory vanished as my eye caught something. It was a red french fries container stuck in the ice in a marshy area. I grumbled at the teens' lack of reverence—and at my own helplessness to know how to stop them without being unduly mean—and climbed off my rock to retrieve the offending litter. I had taken only two steps when I felt an itch in my chest. It was just a dull itch, as if a bug had made its way through my three layers of clothes to give me a bite. I reached up to scratch. That's when I slipped on a nasty bit of ice and fell.

I don't remember clearly what happened next, but I think my head hit a rock.

I felt so foolish that I laughed out loud. I struggled to my feet and only then realized that I wasn't on my feet at all. I was, in fact, still lying there, half on the shore, half on the fractured ice, my eyes staring upward at the gray December sky.

You may have a few questions at this point. So do I. Dying didn't give me instant knowledge about the secrets of the universe, as I'd hoped it would. I'm a little disappointed about that. Right now all I can say is that time and space seem skewed, which makes sense—I mean, I've always believed that eternity is supposed to be *outside* of time. So when I say, "I died this morning," I don't know if it was really this morning or last week or last year or eons ago. For all I know, everything I'm now seeing may be echoes of time past—like the fading, ancient light from a distant star.

All of this is terribly befuddling for a relaxed Baptist like myself. Because I made a heartfelt profession of faith at

the age of eleven after Brother Walter DuBois's week-long revival at Grace Baptist Church, I thought I would go to heaven when I died. Maybe I have. Or this might be somewhere my theology can't put its finger on. Speculation about the afterlife—even theological speculation—has always been risky, since no one has ever come back to confirm it.

Another thought occurs to me. In recent years, I haven't gone to church as often as I used to. I became a relaxed Baptist after Kathryn died, you see. In a way I was a little miffed at God for taking her away from me. But I knew, as I'm sure he knew, that it was mostly an excuse to get out of the deacons' meetings, choir practices, Sunday school lessons, and Bible studies I'd taken on over the years. Who was going to argue with a grieving widower? But now I wonder if I had played the miffed-at-God role a little too diligently. Should I be worried?

Apparently not, because I feel strangely at peace, wherever I am. I have a profound sense that what I've always believed about the afterlife is still true. Where am I? I'm *here*. Somewhere in eternity.

Without meaning to, I went to see my son Jonathan. I'm not sure how it happened. I merely thought of him—wondered how he would take the news of my death—and suddenly I was in his apartment. I had never seen his apartment when I was alive, mind you. It was in Baltimore, which was too far away, and long drives made me nauseous. Besides that, he had never invited me to come. Yet there I stood in a depressing, single-room studio with a tiny icebox and stove, card table and folding chair, a bed, and a dresser—

and I *knew* it was Jonathan's apartment. I can't say *how* I knew it, but I did.

Little wonder he hadn't asked me to visit. I would have been terribly upset if I'd known he was living in these conditions. A roach skittered across the counter. The wallpaper was water-stained and peeling. The carpet, which was worn through to the bare floor in patches, smelled of mildew.

A small alarm clock said it was seven minutes past five. I had been dead for eight hours—*if* this was the same day I died. In any event, the sun was gone (though I wondered if the sun's rays ever reached this tenement, nestled as it was—how do I know these things?—between two larger apartment buildings).

I heard a key slip into the lock. A moment later, Jonathan Lee, my second son, walked in. He looked around wearily as if the sight of the apartment was as offensive to him as it was to me. He was bundled in a winter coat his mother had given to him five years ago. It looked the worse for wear. He wore a hard hat, and his jeans were covered in dry-wall dust. His face, a masculine version of Kathryn's, was lean and stubbled. He looked older than his twenty-eight years, tired and sad. That bothered me. He tossed the hard hat onto the bed. His brown hair was cropped short. He'd had a ponytail last time I saw him. When was that? Last summer when he came to visit on his way to a Steelers game.

He dropped his coat on the bed, crossed to the sink, and made some coffee. He stared for a moment out the small window. It looked into an alley. While the coffee brewed, he wandered to the far wall beyond the bed. An easel I hadn't noticed stood there, between the bed and the wall. He lifted the tarp covering the easel. I caught a glimpse of a sketch but couldn't make out the details.

I felt relieved—if that's the right word in my current state. At least he was still drawing, if not actually painting. He was so gifted as an artist, but he'd changed a lot in the past couple of years. In fact, he had said that he'd given up on art. Why? On the one occasion he'd dignified my question with an answer, he'd said he was suffering from "artist's block." Then he'd made it clear that was all he intended to say on the subject.

Maybe his "artist's block" had ended. But when he dropped the cover over the easel with a disgusted expression, my relief vanished.

A phone rang beside the bed. Jonathan stared at it as if he might not bother to pick it up. I hoped he would. It was Pastor Joshua Bennett himself—although how I knew that so certainly I couldn't really say. Maybe it was because the call related to my death.

On the sixth ring, Jonathan snatched up the receiver. "Hello?" he said.

Pastor Joshua told him the news in that sweet, gentle way he has when it comes to bad news. His voice even choked as he spoke.

"I found him by the pond," Pastor Joshua explained. "We were supposed to have lunch together, and when your father didn't show, I went to look for him."

That made me wonder why I hadn't seen Joshua find my body. Why had I been whisked away from seeing his reaction, from watching the ambulance come, from all the things that had happened between then and now?

I could imagine it, though. Poor Josh arriving at the pond, the alarm he must have felt to see me lying there. He and I were best friends, and I was sure that my sudden departure had devastated him, as his death would have devastated me. And, good friend that he was, he'd taken it upon himself to track down my children to break the news to them.

I was momentarily intrigued that he had decided to call Jonathan first. David is the oldest, and I suppose etiquette would have dictated that David be at the top of the list. Yet Pastor Joshua called Jonathan first, just as I'd thought of Jonathan first. Was there a connection? I could only guess that Pastor Joshua knew as I did that Jonathan's fragility as an artist was misleading—he was actually the strongest of my three kids.

After Joshua's heartfelt, jarring explanation, Jonathan slumped onto the bed and rubbed his mouth. "I'll call David and Ruth, then drive up right away," he said, his tongue clicking dryly in his mouth. He hung up the phone and flung himself back on his bed, covering his eyes with his arms. His stillness and the regularity of his breath told me nothing of his emotions. I couldn't even tell whether he was crying. Unfortunately, X-ray vision didn't come with death. But I still *felt* his grief and had *impressions* of his thoughts. They were filled with a sense of loss.

Then I was away again.

David was in a luxurious hotel room in New York when he got the news. I felt badly for him since the phone call came just as he was about to finalize some kind of business deal with an associate. I knew he was on the verge of success because his lips went thin and tight, the way they always had when he was about to foreclose on all of us when we'd played Monopoly as a family. This time was for real, though, and he had just pulled some papers out of his briefcase, drawn a gold pen from his suit-jacket pocket, and handed them to the other gentleman in the room when the phone rang. Like Jonathan, David almost let the phone ring unanswered. But the other man wouldn't sign the contracts because the ringing distracted him. David sensed his annoyance and grabbed the phone.

When he heard Jonathan's voice, he excused himself and used the phone in the bathroom—it was one of those classy hotels that had one there and only God knows why. Closing the door, he gently dropped the lid on the toilet and sat down. He listened to Jonathan for a moment, asked a few questions to make sure he had the details right, then said he would fly there as soon as he could. He placed the receiver back on the cradle and stood up. Lowering his head, he steadied himself on the sink counter. He took a deep breath, then looked at himself in the bathroom mirror. His round face—uncannily like Kathryn's brother Stan, except with my eyes—had gone pale. He ran his fingers through his perfectly cut black hair, turned to the door, then paused as if to decide whether he could return to his business associate. His fingers poised above the knob for a moment. They began to tremble.

David is the opposite of Jonathan. He puts on a very convincing strong-man act, but inside he's soft and weak. He sat down on the toilet lid again, shoved a washcloth into his mouth to stifle any noise, and wept. I wanted to comfort him. I even tried to touch his heaving shoulders and couldn't.

The artificial glow of the bathroom light in David's hotel room suddenly dimmed and I was in a cozy darkness. Did I will myself there? No. But there I was nonetheless, sitting in a chair in my daughter's apartment, the silhouettes of her meager pieces of furniture crudely outlined by a hall light she'd left on. I heard voices on the other side of the front door, loud and laughing, and then the door itself opened and a small crowd of people swarmed in. A young man they called Jeffrey fumbled for the light switch and nearly knocked a picture off the wall.

"Be careful," Ruth said as she closed the door behind her.

The dozen young people—all in their early twenties like her—were her friends, but I had the immediate feeling that she didn't really like them very much. They spread out into the apartment and immediately made themselves at home, chatting happily and guffawing at jokes I didn't understand. One attractive girl with deep dimples giggled and then stumbled, bumping the small Christmas tree Ruth had set up in the corner. The balls and bells clinked and jingled.

"Be *careful*," Ruth said again as she moved to the small kitchen, partitioned from the living room by a counter and overhanging cupboards. "I'm making coffee. Who wants some?"

A dark-haired boy with a loose tie and superficial lust for the girl with the dimples complained, "I want something to drink."

"Coffee *is* a drink," my daughter replied in a flat, nononsense tone she'd inherited from her mother. Her friends carried on with their reveling, oblivious to her, her tone, and her coffee. I sensed that most of these people were coworkers with whom she'd just been to a Christmas party. One couple—a blond-haired boy and a rather heavyset girl—fell onto the couch and whispered conspiratorially about sneaking into the bedroom. They were married, but not to each other. Someone turned on the stereo. A saxophone played "Jingle Bells" to a throbbing beat.

A boy in an oddly festive sport coat of red and green tried to sit on me, so I got up and walked over to the corner next to a large plastic version of a houseplant. It had a coating of dust on it. My daughter hadn't inherited her mother's house-cleaning skills.

Ruth drifted around the counter and went to the large window in her makeshift dining area. Pushing the curtain aside, she stared sadly at the Pittsburgh skyline and the snow that had just begun to fall on it. I didn't remember snow being in the forecast again. She sighed and folded her arms.

I'm tempted to say that she looked as beautiful as my wife, Kathryn. That would be sentimental. The truth is, Ruth is more beautiful than Kathryn was. Somehow she'd been blessed with the best features from both sides of the family. Large hazel eyes set upon perfectly round cheeks, a dainty nose and full lips, and brown hair that fell magically into place no matter how many times she ran her fingers through it. A tall, slender but shapely build that drew men's glances no matter where she was or what she wore. My daughter, I say as objectively as possible, is worthy of a poet's raptures or a painter's eye.

A dark-haired boy named Terry came up behind her and wrapped his arms around her waist. He kissed her on the neck. "What's so interesting?" he asked.

My heart sank as I knew—in this strange way that I seemed to know things in my present condition—that my daughter had slept with this boy, not out of love but out of loneliness, and even now she regretted it. He was the kind who talked about it at the office to his workmates, and she had realized that too late. He now feigned affection, not as a lover but as a conqueror. I knew all of this as surely as if I'd been told directly by both Ruth and Terry.

She slipped from Terry's grasp and made her way back to the kitchen. "Coffee," she said, as if that answered his question.

He smiled indulgently. I had the rather coarse and earthy desire to knock the smirk off his face.

Ruth was pouring the coffee when the phone at the end of the counter rang. I knew it was Jonathan.

"It's the neighbors!" the whispering boy from the couch suddenly shouted. He thought the exclamation was funny, though no one else did.

Putting down the coffeepot, Ruth reached for the phone, her elbow brushing one of the mugs and knocking it over. The coffee spilled. She swore mildly. "Get the phone, will you, Terry?" she cried out as she quickly grabbed some paper towels to mop up the mess.

"Hello?" Terry said. "Yeah, she's right here. Who's this?"

Ruth ducked behind the counter to clean up wayward drops of coffee. Terry cupped his hand over the phone and said, "Some guy named Jonathan."

Ruth reappeared, still clutching the soggy paper towel, her expression already a mixture of fear and worry. She took the phone from Terry, but she instinctively knew the worst before Jonathan had a chance to say anything. Leaning onto the counter, her left elbow touched the edge of a small puddle of spilled coffee and soaked into the fabric of her sweater. She struggled to hold back the tears. She didn't want to cry in front of this crowd. More important, she didn't want Terry to have an excuse to touch her in the name of comfort.

"What's wrong?" Terry asked, after she'd hung up the phone.

Ruth converted her grief to anger. "Tell everyone to get out."

"What?" Terry was clearly surprised—not that she wanted everyone to leave, but that she could speak so harshly. I wished she'd spoken to him this clearly before.

"Tell everyone to get out," she said. "My father is dead."

Nothing throws cold water on a party like an obituary announcement. It was an indication of this crowd's level of friendship that no one offered to stay to help or console her. Terry had the nerve to pout. His plan to sleep with my daughter later that night had been foiled. That alone made me think my death was worthwhile. They all filed out like cattle in expensive coats.

My daughter wept uncontrollably. As with David, I reached out to her but could not penetrate the barrier of time and space, flesh and spirit.

Pastor Joshua once speculated that hell wasn't going to be a *place* as much as it was going to be a *situation*—one of endless separation. As I watched my little girl cry, I felt sure that I was in hell.

Two

I'm aware of time. Not of its passing, but of its absence. It's a strange adjustment. I now have to concentrate very hard on the markers, the means by which I used to measure the passing of time. I'm not talking about watching the hands move on a clock, or a digital number kick over. I mean the literal activities that move time forward: the time it took Ruth to pack, walk to her car, get in, and drive out of Pittsburgh and south on the turnpike to my house in her hometown. For her, it took nearly two hours (not counting the stop for coffee at Gleason's Diner). For me, it didn't "take" any time at all. I was detached from her sensation of time—and my own. In that sense, it's similar to a "dissolve" in a movie, fading out the scene in her apartment and focusing in on a new scene: Ruth standing next to my undecorated Christmas tree at home. But even a film-like "dissolve" indicates a passing of time. Now the words fail me. I know only that eternity is not time without end, but rather the *absence* of time. It simply isn't here to count, measure, or consider.

21

Were I not witnessing my loved ones who are trapped *in* time, I would not even think about it—except perhaps as a vague, half-remembered notion.

Ruth also thought about time as she stood in the center of my living room. But for her, the feeling was that time had stopped. The Sears Victorian-replica couch and matching love seat, the plush easy chair, the gold lamps, end tables, imitation classic paintings, and photos on the walls and mantel above the small brick fireplace—these had been unchanged for as long as Ruth could remember. Kathryn and I had not been conscious of fashion or trends. We bought furniture that we hoped would be durable. We decorated our home modestly, from both our sense of taste and our budgetary constraints. (My publishing ventures were rarely profitable.) If nothing else, we were consistent. When the kids came home to visit, which they rarely did, it was to a familiar place. We thought they needed at least one constant in their tumultuous lives: the home where they grew up.

After Kathryn died, I got all kinds of suggestions from family and friends about the house. Some thought I should move. Some said I should rearrange things, get new furniture, make adjustments, all to keep from being reminded of her in my grief. I felt the opposite. I wanted to keep everything just as it was so I would be reminded of her when my grief subsided.

Ruth stood before my undecorated Christmas tree in her winter coat. "Oh, Daddy," she said sadly. She took her coat off and dropped it onto the couch and hummed "Blue Christmas" without knowing why. I knew. Her eye had caught my cassette of Elvis's Christmas album sitting on the end table. I had played it while bringing the boxes of Christmas decorations down from the attic. That song—one of his most memorable—had slipped in to her subconscious and out through her hummings.

She heard the subdued roar of Jonathan's Volkswagen van pull up. Like her younger self, she skipped to the door and pulled it open just as Jonathan stepped onto the porch.

"Hiya," he said as he dropped his suitcase and gave her a long hug in the yellow glow of the porch light. The snow had followed Ruth from Pittsburgh and now fell behind them in the darkness.

"Jonathan," Ruth cried, then buried her face in his shoulder and sobbed.

He guided her into the house. "You'll freeze your tears if we stay out here," he said, then retrieved his suitcase and closed the door.

She shook her head. "I can't believe it. I talked to him a week ago . . . he was fine . . . and then . . . I just can't believe it."

"I know," Jonathan said and handed her a tissue.

She dabbed at her eyes, careful not to smear what was left of her makeup. "He didn't say anything about heart problems. Doc Mason said he was strong as a bull at his last checkup. How can you have a heart attack when you're strong as a bull?"

This was news to me. A heart attack? I'd died of a heart attack? Is that what the itch in my chest was?

What a relief. A fatal heart attack I could cope with. Killing myself by slipping on a rock was humiliating.

Ruth continued. "Mason thought it was because he carried the tree in with Billy Atkinson, then he brought all the boxes down from the attic."

"By himself?" Jonathan asked.

"By himself."

When did she get all this information? I wondered. Had she called Pastor Joshua when I couldn't see her? Again, what I saw—and *didn't* see—was beyond my control.

"Somebody should've been here," Ruth said. And I knew she thought that that somebody should have been her. Guilt welled up with her tears. Of the three, Ruth had the least to feel guilty about where I was concerned. She was the most conscientious about phone calls and visits.

"Drop it, Ruth," Jonathan said gently. "Don't do this to yourself."

She nodded, not wholeheartedly taking his advice. "David left a note in the kitchen."

"He made it already? That was fast."

Ruth half-smiled. "He has means of flight that we mere mortals don't. He's with Pastor Joshua at the funeral home." She sat down on the couch next to her coat and tucked her legs underneath her like Kathryn used to. Blowing her nose, she stared vacantly.

Jonathan lingered near the Christmas tree, gently touching one of the ornaments.

"How are things in Baltimore?" Ruth asked.

He shrugged. "Same old stuff. I'm foreman now."

"What does that mean?"

"I get to wear a different color hard hat than the rest of the guys. Sometimes I boss them around—when they let me. Is there any coffee?" He walked off to the kitchen before she could answer. By the sounds of the banging cupboard doors, Ruth hadn't yet made any and he was trying to find the means to make some.

Ruth waited a moment, knew he'd forgotten where I kept things, then went in to rescue him. At the counter, she nudged him aside and asked, "Any new paintings?" She tried to make it sound like a casual question.

Jonathan shook his head. "Not much time for that kind of thing. What about you? You're still one of those secretaries . . ."

"Administrative assistant," she corrected him.

"For a travel agency . . ."

"Bank."

"In Pittsburgh."

Ruth smiled. "Right. One out of three isn't bad."

I was surprised. My son and my daughter seemed to know very little about each other's lives. They spoke as mere acquaintances at a forced reunion. Until this moment, I had thought—well, *hoped*—that they kept in touch with each other, if not with me.

"Do you like it?"

The coffeemaker choked and gurgled. Ruth leaned against the counter. "It's not a career, if that's what you mean."

"What is it, then?"

"I don't know," she said. "I don't know what I want to do. I work hard during the week for my fun on the weekends. That's the extent of my life—neatly summarized."

"Hmm," Jonathan said thoughtfully. "Working for the weekends? That must be why you look so tired."

Ruth touched her face and eyes self-consciously. "Do I look tired? Oh no, I can't. I don't want anyone in this town to think I'm anything but happy and healthy and carefree."

Jonathan laughed.

Ruth tried to look at her reflection on the polished side of the toaster. "All I need is Jan Binnocek yapping about how the big city is wearing me out."

"Why should you care what Jan Binnocek—or *anybody*—says?" Jonathan frowned.

"Because ... well, *because*," Ruth replied, as if the second "because" should answer his question. It didn't. Jonathan merely gazed at her. She explained further: "You know how they were when I left. 'Oh, there goes little Miss Prima Donna—off to the big city for fame and fortune.'" For this last quote, Ruth put her hands on her hips and did a reasonably good impression of Nancy Melville, the busybody who worked at the Quick Stop grocery store on Gallatin Avenue.

Jonathan raised an eyebrow. "Fame and fortune? That why you left?"

"No."

"Oh," Jonathan said, then added wryly, "that's why *I* went."

The coffee was ready. Ruth retrieved two mugs from the rack beside the refrigerator. Jonathan looked chagrined as she sat them on the counter. Both mugs had icons of Elvis on them. One was a head shot of him as a young man with his "hound-dog" expression; the other came from his white-sequined-jumpsuit-in-Las-Vegas period. The former mug was mine, the latter had belonged to my wife. Jonathan poured the coffee, and I knew he would later claim the mugs for his own.

"I just wanted to get out of here. Is that so terrible? To try to make something of myself outside Peabody's city limits?" Ruth yanked open the refrigerator door to pull out some half-and-half. I tried to remember how fresh it was. When had I last gone shopping?

Jonathan smiled patiently at her. "You're pleading your case to the wrong person, Ruth." I seemed to hear the rest of what he *didn't* say to her: *I was the promising young artist who would make a name for himself in New York's great art exhibits. I made a name, all right. I went from canvas to dry-wall in record time. And to top it off, I never made it to New York.*

Ruth sighed.

"Eh," Jonathan said with a dismissive hand. It was one of my gestures. "When do things ever go according to plan? Life isn't paint-by-number."

I was genuinely perplexed by the strangeness of their conversation. Had they really not talked at all in the time since they'd moved away from home? An uneasy feeling needled at my consciousness. My perceptions of my children's lives had obviously not been accurate. Had I been kidding myself about their relationships?

Then I wondered, Is this what death does? Does it bring clarity? Are the delusions and carefully contrived fantasies we have formed in life stripped away in death? Am I now seeing things as they *really* are?

Jonathan and Ruth returned to the living room. Ruth sat down on the couch again and sipped her coffee, while Jonathan slipped into my easy chair. They were silent and, apart from the underlying unfamiliarity between them, the scene looked cozy. The two of them hadn't been together in my living room like that since Kathryn's death. I longed to be with them—in the flesh, I mean—to share it. And the irony that *my* death had made this moment possible was not lost on me.

Two cars pulled up outside. I recognized the sound of one, an American Motors Rambler that belonged to Pastor Joshua Bennett. Jonathan and Ruth also heard the cars but didn't move. They watched the door to see if whoever it was would knock or simply walk in. The door opened and two men walked in: Joshua and my elder son, David.

Joshua looked bad. His slender, weathered face showed a hint of uncharacteristic stubble that gave him the look of a man having a terrible hangover. His blue eyes were red-rimmed. His white hair was disheveled, his lean body stooped. My death hung on him like chains.

David, on the other hand, looked perfectly groomed. The son I'd seen crying in a hotel bathroom was now composed and in control. There was business to be taken care of, and nobody could take care of it like my David.

Pastor Joshua, Jonathan, and Ruth embraced and greeted each other warmly. Ruth started to cry again, and I thought Joshua would join her. But he shook his head suddenly and said, "Ah, Ruth, Ruth. It's all right. Plenty of time for that later."

Meanwhile David shook Jonathan's hand and received a quick hug from Ruth. It looked clumsy and awkward. I wasn't surprised. David neither gave nor took affection very well. He perceived it as a sign of weakness. Weak people often do.

"I was wondering when you two would arrive," David said. "What did you do, come by camel?"

"A camel would have been faster than the way I came," Jonathan replied.

"And not all of us have our own jets," Ruth reminded him with a playful jab.

"Ruth, you are a rose in winter," Pastor Joshua said as he took Ruth's hand and stepped back. "Let me look at you!"

Ruth blushed and smiled at him.

"Ah, if I were twenty years younger ..." he said.

"She'd still have to be twenty years older," David said.

"You look wonderful," Pastor Joshua said. "A little tired, perhaps, but wonderful."

Ruth self-consciously touched her face and eyes again.

"This town—our church—hasn't been the same without you." His eyes swept past the three of them. "Without all of you."

"So how did it go?" Jonathan asked, obviously changing the subject.

David tugged at his leather gloves to get them off. "The pastor and I were at the funeral home."

"You said in your note." Ruth chewed on her lower lip nervously. "Did you ... did you see Dad?"

"Yes," David said without elaborating. "All the details are taken care of."

"Details?" Ruth asked.

"The funeral home. The business arrangements."

Jonathan looked coolly at David. "Business."

"Yes, *business*. The McWilliams Funeral Home is a business like anything else."

Jonathan stiffened. "And I'm sure you negotiated soundly, squeezed out every penny, got to the bottom line, and struck the best deal on behalf of our father."

"Jonathan . . ." Ruth said in a low, admonishing tone.

Ever the diplomat, Joshua said, "There was a lot that needed doing, Jonathan."

Jonathan didn't respond.

Shoving his gloves into his coat pockets, then slipping out of the coat itself, David seemed to ignore Jonathan's attitude. "Whether it's funerals, building houses, or selling cotton candy, business is business. Mr. McWilliams knows that, and so do I. You can't blame me for making sure we aren't taken advantage of."

"You make it sound like you were haggling over a new car," Jonathan said unhappily.

David shrugged. "If you want to go back and make some other arrangements with Mr. McWilliams, feel free."

"Not me," Jonathan said, an edge to his voice. "You're the wheeler-dealer. If you say you got the best deal, then heaven forbid that I say otherwise."

"Then what's wrong?"

"Nothing."

"Good."

"Good."

"Coffee?" Pastor Joshua asked, sniffing the air.

"In the kitchen," Jonathan said.

"I'll get it," David said and strode out.

Pastor Joshua turned his attention to Ruth once more. "You know, I never found anyone to take over your Sunday school class. The department's gone downhill in the three years since you left. Those poor kids. They've missed you so much."

Ruth's eyes narrowed. "I don't believe you. Those little delinquents celebrated the day I left."

"Not true!" Joshua protested. "And they're not the only ones who miss you. Ted Hagan asked me to pass along his greetings and condolences."

"Little *Teddy* Bear?" David called from the kitchen. "I thought he moved after he got his degree."

"Not every young person in this town felt obligated to leave us, David," Pastor Joshua said.

"Ted's very sweet," Ruth said with a noncommittal politeness. "Thank him for me."

"You can thank him yourself. He hopes to see you while you're here, if you have a chance. Maybe you could stop by his office when you're out and about—if you think it's appropriate, all things considered." Joshua never let incidentals like a death or a funeral get in the way of his matchmaking. He watched Ruth carefully for her reaction. She was poker-faced.

David returned from the kitchen. "Ted has an office at the Park 'n Dine? Worked his way up from the milkshake maker, huh?"

"He's assistant manager at the bank now," Joshua said to David, but kept his gaze on Ruth. "He's shy about you, Ruth."

Ruth frowned. "We dated for three years, Pastor. Why would he be shy about me?"

"He thinks living in Pittsburgh has changed you," Joshua explained. "You're not the girl he dated in high school. You're a sophisticated working woman now."

"Ha," David interjected.

"If I get a chance, I'll look him up," Ruth said, then turned away from Joshua and feigned interest in my undecorated Christmas tree. Pastor Joshua spoke with Jonathan about another "bit of business," and David drank his coffee indifferently. They didn't see the tears slip down Ruth's face. She cleverly wiped them away without anyone knowing she was crying at all. I had the feeling she'd become quite good at hiding her feelings. Sadly, I also had the feeling that these tears were not for me, but for the secrets she knew she had to keep from Jonathan, David, Pastor Joshua, Ted, and everyone else in Peabody. She had changed, all right, but she didn't like *how* she'd changed.

"Jonathan, there's something we need to talk about. It can wait until morning if you're tired from your drive," Pastor Joshua was saying when I turned my attention back to him.

David took another sip of his coffee, but his gaze at Jonathan was steadfast. He knew what Pastor Joshua was about to say. I didn't.

Jonathan looked at the two men warily. "What? Tell me now. I'm not tired."

"I was wondering when you have to be back in Baltimore," Joshua said.

Jonathan shrugged. "That depends on what needs doing here. Why?"

"It's something your father wanted," Joshua said carefully. "It was one of his 'last requests.' He mentioned it to me several times and, as a witness to his will, I know it's in there, too."

"I'm not sure I like the sound of this," said Jonathan.

To be honest, neither did I. My mind was blank about any "last requests" regarding Jonathan.

Joshua cleared his throat, glanced at David, then back at Jonathan. "He wanted you to paint something special for the church. Maybe even for Christmas. In his memory. We'll make a plaque to go with it."

Oh, that's right. I had forgotten all about the idea. I wanted Jonathan to paint something for the church in memory of Kathryn and me. Being a traditional old church, filled with plaques, donated stained-glass windows, pews, pulpits, rooms—even the tea service for the Ladies' Reading Club was a gift—I thought a painting from Jonathan would be appropriate. I had mentioned it to Joshua several years ago, when I wrote my will, and had since put it out of my mind because of Jonathan's later disposition.

"You're joking," Jonathan said.

"Not at all."

Jonathan stammered, "But—it can't be done. I can't just toss together a painting in time for Christmas."

"When you were living here you could!" Joshua protested. "That painting you did for the new meeting hall is still there—and you put that one together in less than a week. I remember! We thought it was a miracle. Still do."

Jonathan slumped onto the edge of the couch. "Those kinds of miracles don't happen anymore."

Joshua studied him silently, then said, "You don't have to answer right this minute. Just think about it."

Ruth sat down next to Jonathan. "Do it for Daddy, Jonathan. It's what he wanted."

Jonathan shook his head slowly.

"I told you," David said to Joshua.

Joshua looked helplessly at Jonathan, who now looked up at his older brother. "What?"

"I told him you wouldn't do it."

"What made you so sure I wouldn't?"

"It's obvious, isn't it?"

Jonathan leaned forward. "Is it? Tell me what's obvious, David."

David looked at him impatiently. "You're afraid to try. You know you wouldn't finish it by Christmas, or Easter, or next Halloween, for that matter."

"You're goading me," Jonathan said. "You're *daring* me."

David shrugged and drank some more coffee. Silence hung over them like a wet blanket.

Finally Joshua said, "Well, I'm just the messenger of your father's request. Nothing says you have to do it."

"I just don't think it's possible. Not in such a short amount of time, what with the funeral and all."

Pastor Joshua left it at that and said good night. At the door, he hesitated, then added, "It's good to have you here—the children of Richard Lee all together again. People in this town loved him a lot. *I* loved him, as you know. He was a good man."

I thanked him for the impromptu eulogy, but he didn't hear me. He stepped into the cold night.

As Joshua's cold car engine roared to life, I got some very distinct impressions of my children's thoughts, as if they were sending me wordless messages. Their thoughts came to me like waves of electricity. What I "received" was disturbing—particularly since they were thinking about me.

Through Jonathan, I saw myself as he saw me: a fatherly artistic impresario, one who had encouraged him in his painting with unceasing enthusiasm. That much was true. I'd been proud of my son's talent and affirmed it whenever I could. But piggybacked onto that feeling was a darker, more oppressive perception: Jonathan felt that he was a failure in my eyes for not fulfilling his artistic potential. His "artist's block" had put a wedge between us, he thought. He feared that I had spent the past few years lamenting his lack of productivity and vision.

I had no time to react, because Ruth's thoughts suddenly invaded my sensibilities. To her I was a gentle, loving, small-town man who'd been disappointed in her for leaving our small-town life in favor of big-city freedom. And along with the burden of guilt she carried for "disappointing" me, she was awash in guilt for the decisions she had made to get as far along in her big-city life as she had. I thought of Terry, the boy-conqueror at her apartment, and suspected that he was only one of many who—

My thought was interrupted; suddenly David's perceptions hit me with the full power of a bolt of lightning (and as one who was once struck by lightning, I would know). *The people in this town loved him all right. He was a pushover for anything they wanted,* David thought.

The deep cynicism of the thought startled me.

And then the images came. One after another in a succession of memories: the Saturday mornings I had spent helping with maintenance at the church, the evenings I had left home to visit someone who was bedridden or in the hospital, the pocket money I had given to those who came to the door for a handout or were destitute on the street. The charities, the civic organizations, the fund-raisers. *The time and the money*, David thought. *The time and the money . . .*

In David's mind, I was generous to a fault—giving and compassionate—but a gullible fool. A sucker to every worthless cause and charity that Peabody had to offer.

"David—wait just a minute," I said, wanting to correct him—to correct them all. But no one could hear me.

Ruth pressed a tissue to her nose and sniffled. "He was a good man—and a good father."

"He was the best," Jonathan concurred.

David didn't say a word.

Three

Jonathan's bedroom was in the attic. He had announced, as a teenager, that it appealed to his sense of artistry to move off the second floor where the rest of us slept and get into a "loft" of his own. Kathryn and I wanted to encourage his muse, so we obliged him.

Now, as an adult, he looked at the room with a mixture of embarrassment and lost hope. Little had changed since he moved away. The only adjustment to the room's decor was the increase in Elvis paraphernalia: photos, magazines, statuettes, pewter figurines, collectible records, an Elvis clock with "swiveling hips" instead of a pendulum. Our inventory ranged from the tastefully luxurious to the blatantly tacky. I had moved the Elvis "collection" to Jonathan's room after Kathryn's death. Actually, Jonathan had insisted on it—he considered me a "fickle fan," whereas he and his mother were die-hard, true-to-the-end believers. I couldn't argue. Kathryn had loved Elvis. Not with the fanatical love of the "Elvis is still alive" disciples,

37

to be sure, but he had touched her heart in a way no other musician or celebrity ever had. She often said that there was something about his music—about *him*—that made her feel alive. I knew for a fact that she had gone out with me in the first place because I reminded her of him.

That was intentional on my part. A mutual friend had told me what a big fan she was, so I made sure to wear my hair like he did. We saw *Blue Hawaii* on our first date. When she learned that Elvis and I shared the exact same birth date, we were as good as engaged. When I informed her that I had served *with* Elvis in the army at Fort Chaffee and Fort Hood in 1958—and was in on the football game that broke one of his fingers—marriage was a mere formality.

I was a fan, too. I can confess to being awestruck by him when we first met in the army. We ate together at the canteen, went on bivouac, and learned about tanks as part of our basic training. He was always friendly and polite and took our teasing about his fame good-naturedly. He was also a dutiful son who called his mother nearly every night and, later that summer, was devastated by her sudden death from hepatitis.

I suddenly remember something I haven't thought of in years: When he came back to the fort to finish his basic training, I bumped into him one evening outside the bunkhouse. He looked worn out. I asked how he was coping with his grief.

"Do you believe the dead can see what the living are doing?" he asked me, point blank.

"I don't know."

"I do," he said. "She can see me now. No more secrets from her. She can see *everything*."

For a moment I thought he was comforted by the idea, then quickly realized that it terrified him. He walked away, his head hung low. That was the last conversation I had with him.

Jonathan was right: I was a fickle fan. As much as I had liked Elvis as a person, I thought his best years ended with the advent of the Beatles. After that, something changed for him. It was as if he lost his way. The easy, obvious explanation was that he fell into the hands of corporate mercenaries and went commercial, making bad movies and mediocre music.

I believed that the reason for Elvis's decline was less obvious: Something happened to him in much deeper places. What, exactly, I couldn't say. So, where Kathryn had adored him to the bitter end, I clung instead to his earliest incarnation. She mourned his death; I felt sorry for his lost potential.

Jonathan followed his mother's lead (and love) and took Elvis as his role model. I teased him that it wouldn't help his painting. He argued that it would, that the essence of creativity in any art form was the same. I couldn't disagree, since I also believed that all creativity comes from the same source: the soul, our meeting-place with God.

Tossing his suitcase onto the bed, Jonathan scanned the room. Behind a life-size cardboard cutout of young Elvis, he found his old art supplies, sketch pads, and unfinished paintings. He sat down at his student desk and looked through a scrapbook of his very first drawings that Kathryn had kept for him.

Once again, I "saw" images and felt impressions from him—so vividly that I couldn't tell if they were his memories or my own.

I see him as a small boy, showing me some drawings he had made.

"See, Dad? This is Mrs. McGinty's cow out in the field," he says.

And there is my younger self smiling. "This is wonderful, son. And what is this next to her, a scarecrow?"

"No!" he protests. "That's Mrs. McGinty!"

I laugh, but proudly. "A perfect likeness."

Then I see another day, a few years later. He is holding up a picture he had drawn that morning.

"This is what you drew in Sunday school today?" I ask.

"Uh-huh. It's Jesus healing a blind man," my eight-year-old says excitedly. He is serious now—and wants to be taken seriously. He is no longer a child who wants to be a fireman one week and the president the next. His mind is set: he wants to be an artist. And I remember that it was his early attempts to draw Jesus' miracles in Sunday school that stirred his artist's heart. I suspect there is something inside every artist that wants to capture the miraculous, the eternal, in his or her work.

"I see the blind man. But why can't we see Jesus' face?" I ask earnestly.

Jonathan looks perplexed, then frowns. "It's because *I* can't see Jesus' face. I . . . can't see it in my head," he replies sadly.

Then I hear myself saying to him, "That's all right, son. In the movie *Ben-Hur* we never see Jesus' face either."

He looks at me silently. He knows I'm being conde-scending in a well-intentioned fatherly way and won't tol-erate it. "Mrs. Ashley says I have to know Jesus in my heart before I can draw his face."

I nod. Mrs. Ashley is his Sunday school teacher, and I wouldn't dream of contradicting her. "Knowing him in your heart is very important, but not just so you can draw him. Remember, a person is more than lines and shadows on canvas."

For me, that was the mystery of art: the intuitive, *spiritual* way a painter or poet or writer or composer can make lines, colors, words, rhymes, and notes come together into a form that speaks of life. One could not be detached from the spiritual realm and be an artist, I often said.

"I can't even do lines and shadows anymore," the adult Jonathan lamented to no one he could see. "All I know is an empty canvas."

Then his feelings came to me like a blast of heat. He considered his life an empty canvas—completely blank. *And what good is an empty canvas?* he mused. *What can you use it for?* Holding up his sketch pad this way and that, he pondered the question. *You could use it as a table, a window shutter, a modernistic hat, a bookend.* His mind raced on in a frenzied stream of consciousness. *My paintings could be used as a tray for eggnog, a sled, a candleholder, a Christmas-tree stand . . .*

"An empty canvas is no good until it is used for the purpose it was created to serve," he said, on the edge of a deep sigh. My heart went out to him. For years I had felt like an empty canvas as well, wanting desperately to write, but not having the talent to do it. It was much later—after surrendering to the truth of my limitations—that I became an editor and publisher instead. I found contentment in helping others to write who were better than I was. But Jonathan suffered from no such limitations as a painter. He could do it. I knew he could. I *willed* for him to try.

To my surprise, he picked up an empty sketch pad and started to draw.

Four

Jonathan drew well into the night, not on the sketch pad, but on a spare canvas he'd found in the closet. But had it not been for Ruth's curiosity, I wouldn't have seen what he drew. *Why* I couldn't see it, I don't know. It was as if I stood behind Jonathan while he worked, and his shoulder was always in the way. Like everything else that's happened to me since I died, I can't explain why I see some things with amazing clarity while other things are kept from me.

Ruth peeked in on Jonathan the next morning to see if he wanted anything from town. She had her coat on and a folded newspaper tucked under her arm. Spying the propped-up canvas only half-covered, she silently lifted aside the cover and sneaked a peek. It was a rough sketch of a manger surrounded by countless unidentified figures. A nativity scene? Was that his sudden inspiration? But the crowd surrounding the manger was too large for any of the traditional accounts of the birth of Christ. The angels and the shepherds? It was too early to know.

Jonathan stirred and Ruth quickly dropped the cover onto the canvas. "Good morning," she said, turning to him as he rolled over to face her.

"Hi."

She tossed the folded newspaper onto the bed. "Dad's obituary is in the paper this morning."

Jonathan stretched and picked up the paper. An old black-and-white photo was at the bottom of the front page alongside a caption announcing that one of Peabody's leading lights had died. I cringed. This was obviously the work of Patricia Kinney, a romance writer wannabe who wrote features for the paper. I glanced at the article—yes, there was the overblown, overwritten style that was Patricia's hallmark. I thought, *If I'm allowed to haunt anyone in my current state, then I might visit her tonight.*

"Need anything from town?" Ruth asked.

Jonathan rubbed his eyes. "Yeah, but I'll have to go myself later. Why are you going?"

"I have to order flowers for the funeral. It's the one thing David didn't feel confident handling."

"Flowers are too abstract for David."

Ruth chuckled, started to leave, then lingered at the door. "How do I look? Do I still look tired?"

Jonathan squinted, trying to focus through his sleepy eyes. "You look good. The heads on Main Street will spin in every direction."

"That sounds horrific," Ruth said, then pretended she'd only just noticed the half-covered canvas. "Oh, what's this?"

Jonathan nearly leapt from the bed to intercept her, but he got tangled in the bedspread. "It's nothing."

She lifted the cover. "I like it. Is this what you're going to paint for the church?"

"Ruth—"

"No, really. I like the way the choir surrounds the manger," she said simply, smiled at him, then left the room.

The choir?

Jonathan sat up, wrapped the blanket around himself, and moved to the canvas. The cardboard cutout Elvis and I watched him curiously.

Jonathan found David downstairs in my study, surrounded by boxes stuffed with my old bank statements and canceled checks. David hammered away at my old adding machine, cursing its stiff keys and archaic technology.

"What are you doing?" Jonathan asked from the doorway.

"It's unbelievable. If you went through these receipts and statements—" The tape in the adding machine jammed up. David tossed up his hands. "I'm telling you, it's unbelievable."

"Dad was a millionaire and didn't know it?"

David tugged and jerked at the machine tape. "You want to know the truth? He gave it all away. If you saw the amounts, you'd realize—" The tape wouldn't cooperate with David's digital fingers. He shoved it aside and dug into his own briefcase for a more modern calculator, then cursed as he realized he'd left it at home.

"Is there coffee on?" Jonathan asked.

"Why did he do it?" David asked as he resumed his entanglement with the tape. "He could've used that money for himself—or us."

Jonathan shrugged. "I don't remember any of us ever needing anything."

David's eyebrows went up. "You're joking. We could've lived in a better house, had nicer clothes. He could have even helped us through college." This last statement was said in a sharp tone.

"I made it okay," Jonathan said. "I had to work hard, but I made it."

"You were only studying art," David said dismissively. "It was a miracle *I* made it—what with accounting and business classes. I got through because of one thing: my scholarships. Scholarships I worked my butt off to get."

David's attitude was getting on my nerves. He had no idea how mistaken he was, but at the same time I felt guilty. Like any parent, I had made a lot of judgment calls about my children over the years, based on who I understood them to be—how I would discipline them, how I would encourage them, how much financial support I would give them. And like any parent, I may have been completely wrong.

"Case in point," David continued. "There are a bunch of checks written out to something called 'the Foster Fund.' Ever heard of it?"

Jonathan shook his head. "What is it?"

"That's the thing: I don't know. But Dad gave them thousands of dollars over the years. It looks like he started donating to this fund when we were in our teens and carried on up to—" He flipped through a stack of recent statements. "Well, the last check was made out a month ago. You don't know what it is?"

"Nope. Never heard of it."

David gestured to my cluttered desk. "That's my point. He gave all this money away to things we don't even know about, all while we had to struggle through school."

Jonathan yawned. "You're the only one complaining, David. Why does it matter so much? You made it, didn't you? You've got more money than you need. What's the problem?"

David leaned forward, resting his elbows on the desk. "It doesn't make sense to me."

"Why does it have to make sense?"

David shot an impatient glance at him. "That's just what I would've expected you to say."

Jonathan ignored the comment. "Can't this wait? Why are you going through Dad's finances now?"

"Because Dad's will left it all to us and I'm the executor. Somebody has to figure out this mess."

Jonathan gazed at him, a telling expression on his face. "And you won't be able to stay after the funeral, right?"

"Right."

"Figures."

David sat silently for a moment. Jonathan sensed that there was something else his brother wanted to say and waited. Then David spoke. "We don't have a choice about some things."

"What?"

"I think we should sell the house."

"Sell the house?" Jonathan and I asked together.

"It'll take care of some of his outstanding bills."

What outstanding bills? The house had been paid off years before; so had the car. I even paid off my credit cards at the end of every month. I was debt free. *What* outstanding bills?

"I think it's a little early to talk about this," Jonathan said.

David misunderstood Jonathan's concern. "We can divide what's left over three ways. Don't worry."

"I'm not worried about the money," Jonathan explained. He was getting annoyed.

"Then what's wrong?"

"This is the house we grew up in."

"So?"

"So—we just lost Dad, and I don't want to think about losing the house, too."

David looked as if Jonathan were speaking in a foreign language. "I don't understand you."

Jonathan groaned. "How could you even *think* about selling it?"

"Easy." David gestured around him. "I mean, just *look at it*. Doesn't it make you feel claustrophobic?"

"You haven't seen my apartment."

David's eyes scanned my study, but he was speaking of the entire house. "I don't have any attachment to this place."

"That's you."

"Are *you* planning to live here, then?"

Jonathan didn't answer the question, but said, "You didn't always feel that way. You loved this house when we were growing up. Just like I did."

David snorted.

"It was a—a castle for us at times. Or a fort in the middle of the wilderness. Don't you remember?"

Suddenly, as if someone switched on a home movie, I see a young David and an even younger Jonathan playing in the living room. Both are dressed in cowboy vests and chaps, with holsters and guns, and moccasins on their feet. They chase each other, waving their guns and shouting, "Bang! Bang!" while using the furniture for cover.

"We had great adventures," I hear the adult Jonathan say, like a voice-over to the scene I see. "You liked to be Daniel Boone."

"Davy Crockett," the adult David corrects him.

The adult Jonathan says, "*I* was Davy Crockett. You liked to be the Texas Ranger."

"Wrong," the adult David says. "You were the Texas Ranger."

"No," the adult Jonathan says.

"Yes. You liked wearing the Texas Ranger hat."

The adult Jonathan grunts. "Maybe I did."

"And I played with the rifle," the adult David says.

"Hold on. No. I had the rifle," says the adult Jonathan.

The two adults now get into an argument about who was who and who owned what, and I smile because the scene is so clear in front of me. And they're so wrong about what they remember. David wears a cowboy hat and holds a pistol while Jonathan wears a coonskin cap and carries a toy rifle.

What am I to make of this? I'm seeing a memory that must be my own—I certainly remember seeing the boys running around like that—yet it was called to my mind in perfect clarity by *their* recollections. And even though they were wrong in what they remembered, I saw it as it really happened. What does it mean?

Slowly, the scene faded to black and I returned to my study.

David sat up in my chair and said firmly, "We were *kids* then, Jonathan. We're not kids anymore, and this place is no castle."

Jonathan wasn't persuaded. "It holds too many memories for us to think about selling."

"Those memories have nothing to do with us now."

"Of course they do."

"Maybe for you," David said.

Jonathan jabbed a finger in the air at David. "For you, too. You're lying to yourself if you say they don't."

"You're going to be my therapist now?"

"No. That would be a bigger job than I could handle."

"Meaning?"

"Meaning that you've turned into something I don't claim to understand."

"Turned *into* something? Like some kind of monster?" David chuckled humorlessly. "Why—because I'm successful? Is that what bugs you?"

"It has nothing to do with success—although you're obviously consumed by it," Jonathan replied. "I'm talking about something else."

"What, then?"

"I'm talking about who you *are*. What you've become."

"What *I've* become? Maybe we should talk about what you *haven't* become."

I flinched on Jonathan's behalf. My two sons glared at each other for a moment.

Jonathan said, "I'm going out."

"Going out for what?" David asked.

"Are we reporting our every movement to you now? Do I need your permission?"

"Just asking."

"Art supplies. Do you mind?"

David smiled sardonically. "Oh. Feeling inspired?"

"No comment," Jonathan growled as he left to get dressed.

"Don't start something you may not be able to finish," David taunted him, then rocked in my chair with a smug expression on his face. If he weren't so old and I weren't so dead, I would've been tempted to spank him.

He resumed his study of the stacks of statements on my desk. He picked up an old check and turned it over and over. "Foster Fund," he said softly.

Five

I don't know exactly when Peabody stopped being a small town and became a "suburb" (as if there's ever a specific date for such transitions), all I can say is that it did. A telltale sign was when the Coliseum Cinema—big-screened, balconied, ornate, and "air conditioned"—closed down because of the multiplex at the new mall. A Pentecostal church rented it for a couple of years, but I sure missed that movie theater. Disney's *The Love Bug* was the last movie screened there. What a way to go.

Just before Thanksgiving I'd heard a rumor that someone wanted to renovate the Coliseum and open it as an "art house" cinema. This gave me hope—until I later learned that Bev Johnson was spreading the rumor because she'd overheard someone tell Wilkie Bell at the diner that "someone should renovate the place and open it as an 'art house' cinema."

That someone was me. I seriously considered doing it myself.

The Coliseum was only one example of how Peabody had changed. There were others. Small shops downtown became government welfare offices. Hayes Department Store, with its five stories, old-fashioned elevator, and red-jacketed operator, succumbed to the chain stores at the mall and the factory outlets on the other side of Brownsville. Hayes was gutted and turned into a flea-market for fly-by-night merchants needing a quick and cheap site to sell their stuff.

Downtown stopped being downtown and Peabody became a suburb, though the word *suburb* usually implies being adjacent to a big city. We're not. Unless you consider Fayetteville a big city, which it isn't. But I believe a town can be a suburb in spirit—and that's what happened to Peabody. It became homogenized—neutered and characterless—to blend in with all the other towns in all the other states. It was inevitable.

But the snowfall from last night somehow made the town look like its former self—reminding me of the old 1950s black-and-white photos of Peabody that George Furnace still has hanging in his dry cleaners. The snow helped to hide the age and neglect. Even the worn-out Christmas decorations that the city has been putting up for years carried a certain charm in spite of the frayed wreaths and the cracked and peeling silver bells and gold chains. I half-expected to see the lights of the Coliseum's marquee lit up again.

Ruth, bundled in her imported coat and scarf, strolled along the main street, a forced smile on her lovely face. She was glad to be back in a familiar place but was intimidated by its potential to make her feel things she didn't want to feel. She said hello to Toni what's-her-name, someone she was on the high-school yearbook committee with. She waved happily to Donna you-know-who, the one that talked behind everybody's back. There was a moment of genuine warmth when Patricia Gnoffo, pushing her twins in a stroller, rounded a corner and nearly knocked Ruth over. They'd never been close friends, but time had made them realize how much they'd liked each other after all. They embraced there on the street. Ruth made a fuss about the twins while Patricia made a fuss about my death, and they parted with promises to meet for coffee whenever Ruth could find the time. Others walked past—mostly people who knew me—to say how sorry they were about my passing. "He's with the Lord now," Dolly Edwards said as she patted Ruth's arm with a wrinkled hand. Ruth was touched.

In Sunshine Florists, Ruth was disheartened to find Jan Binnocek working behind the counter.

"It's so good to see you again," Jan lied. "You look terrific. Maybe a little tired. But losing your father like that must be so hard."

Ruth nodded graciously and asked about flowers for my funeral. Jan pulled out several brochures and plastic-coated catalogues filled with photos of arrangements. Ruth eventually selected an arrangement of lilies to place next to my casket. I never cared much for lilies, but Ruth loved them and, to be candid, I've always thought that the flowers are more for the living than the dead.

Ruth thanked Jan for her help, made no promise about getting together while she was in town, and returned to the crisp Arctic chill outside. Standing in front of the florist shop, Ruth saw the Peabody bank building where

Ted worked. She debated whether to drop by. Her heart said yes, but her pride said no.

The decision was wrenched away from her when Ted himself suddenly appeared next to her. She almost didn't recognize him: he was dressed in a new suit and wore a long cashmere coat. He could've stepped straight out of a *Gentleman's Quarterly* fashion spread.

"Donna Milton came into the bank and said she saw you," Ted smiled sheepishly. He was a good, wholesome-looking boy with sharp blue eyes and curly brown hair. "She said you were buying flowers for your dad. I thought I'd find you here."

"I was just thinking about you." Ruth smiled. "But I hate to bother people when they're working."

"It's no bother. Didn't Pastor Bennett give you my message?"

Ruth nodded. "Yes, he did. But—"

"Do you have a few minutes for some hot chocolate or coffee or—I mean, Michelle's Cafe is still the best on a cold winter's day. If you don't have other errands to run. I know this is a difficult time and there are plenty of things to arrange. I'm going to miss your father . . ." The one thing that bugged me about Ted was his habit of talking too much when he was nervous.

"Let's go to Michelle's," Ruth said. Only I saw the flicker of a real smile on her lips. She thought his nervousness was cute.

They settled at a table in Michelle's. Frank Pierce, the owner, had recently redecorated, getting rid of its contemporary ice-cream-parlor look in favor of a turn-of-the-century "gay nineties" ice-cream-parlor look. I didn't follow his logic, but Frank assured me that his marketing consultant was one of the best in the county. I took his word for it. Regardless of the change, Frank's choice of music was consistent: Elvis's rendition of "The First Noel" came gently over the loudspeakers in the ceiling.

Ruth, meanwhile, was relieved that Michelle's had changed so that she and Ted wouldn't have to awkwardly sit in their "favorite booth," as they had so often after classes. That booth was long gone.

"She started working there . . . oh, a year ago?" Ted said in answer to a question I didn't hear Ruth ask.

"Imagine my surprise. I had no idea Jan Binnocek knew the first thing about flowers," Ruth said, then growled, "She said I look tired."

"She took some kind of night course at the cosmetology school. They're branching out."

"Hair, makeup, and—flowers?"

Ted shrugged. "I guess they figure beauty is beauty, whether human or floral."

"Uh-huh," Ruth said skeptically. "Remind me not to get my hair cut by any of their graduates. They'll turn me into a rhododendron bush."

"The school got an award from some magazine for best hairstyling design. *Better Homes & Gardens*, I think. Want some hot chocolate?"

Ruth nodded. Ted flagged the waitress and ordered for them both. Silence prevailed as they looked around the restaurant. It was empty, except for a lone woman reading a newspaper in the corner.

Ted sighed. "It's not going to be the same, you know."

"What?"

"Peabody without your father." Ted fiddled with a packet of sugar. "He used to meet me here on Wednesday mornings."

Ruth was surprised. "Did you spend a lot of time with him?"

Ted shrugged. "We'd meet here or I'd go over to his house on Friday nights."

"To do what?"

"Oh, we'd talk. Play a board game. Then talk some more." Ted cleared his throat. "He said that just because you and I had broken up, there was no reason I couldn't still be part of the family."

Ruth smiled sadly. "It was very sweet of you to spend time with him. But didn't it cut in on your social life?"

"That *was* my social life," Ted replied.

"Ted. You don't expect me to believe that. I'm sure you have your share of Peabody girls scratching at your door." Ruth paused for a second to think about what she'd just said. "Maybe that wasn't the best expression to use."

"I guess they figured I wasn't worth having after you left me," Ted said sincerely.

Ruth rolled her eyes. "Oh, please."

"You think I'm kidding?"

"I'm not sure I want to know," she said, glancing away as the waitress brought their hot chocolates. Then, "Why don't you tell me about Dad? What did you talk about on your Friday nights together?"

Ted looked at her directly. "You."

Ruth squirmed uncomfortably. "Ted, don't do this."

"You asked," Ted said. "Your father and I both wished you would come home." He took a sip of his hot chocolate, leaving a mustache of white whipped cream above his lip. Without thinking, Ruth reached up with a napkin and wiped it away. He smiled. "Why don't you? Come home, I mean."

"It's not that easy."

"Sure it is."

"No, it isn't," she insisted.

Once again I got certain impressions from my daughter, but they were all tangled up. She felt that she couldn't come home because she didn't think she was *worthy* to come home. She felt guilty for the ways she'd compromised herself in Pittsburgh. *You don't know me, Ted,* she thought. *You think I'm the same girl who left three years ago, but I'm not. You don't know me.*

Ted watched her carefully. "You just make your decision and come home. What's so hard about that?"

"You don't know. Things are complicated. *Life* is complicated."

"Not when you're doing the right thing with your life."

Ruth's anger rose. "That's very cute. Very clever. Is that one of those small-town platitudes you picked up at church?"

"Don't get mad, I just meant that—"

"Tell me something. Why would I want to come back to *Peabody*, of all places?"

"What's wrong with Peabody?" Ted asked defensively.

"It's so . . . so small."

"You have a problem with small towns now?"

I winced. A small town wasn't Ruth's problem. That was merely a diversion. And Ted was falling for it.

"Look at this place!" Ruth went on. "It's depressing. Nobody comes downtown anymore. They're all out at the mall. And it's a second-rate mall, at best."

"So Pittsburgh has first-rate malls. Big deal. Is that your criterion for where you live? Malls? What about family and friendship and community and a sense of belonging—"

"Big cities have those things."

"Maybe they do for some people. How about for you? Are you really happy there? Tell me about your friends in Pittsburgh."

The question startled Ruth. She wondered how much Ted really knew about her life—whether I had guessed at things and passed them on to him during our friendly Friday night conversations. I hadn't, of course. Her life in Pittsburgh had been a mystery to me. But she didn't know that, and it scared her.

"I don't want to talk about this," Ruth said.

Ted immediately retreated. "I'm sorry, Ruth. It's just that—I worry about you. I want to believe you're happy but, at the same time, I hope you aren't. Boy, I'm making a mess of this."

"Ted, Peabody isn't my home anymore. My brothers have moved away, my mother is gone, so is my father now—there's nothing here for me."

Ted stared at his hot chocolate and chewed the inside of his lip. It's what he did when he had something to say but didn't know how to say it; he stared and chewed. I recognized the quirk. So did Ruth.

"I should go," Ruth said and stood up.

Ted also leapt to his feet and nearly knocked the table over in the process. "I'd like to see you again."

"I don't know. We have so much to do. For the funeral. You know."

"I understand," Ted said.

Ruth put on her coat. "Thank you for spending so much time with Dad."

"Your father was good to me," Ted said gently, a hitch in his voice. "It was the very least I could have done."

"It was more than I did," Ruth said, then quickly turned and walked away.

Six

Jonathan also went to town—to the Colorama Art Store—and bought supplies to work on the painting for me. His heart still wasn't in it, but he had an idea, a single compelling idea, and that was more than he'd had in a long time.

I had seen writer's block in a few of the writers I had worked with over the years. It seemed like a remarkably misunderstood phenomenon to me. The problem wasn't that the writer had no ideas. Generally, the writer had plenty of ideas—but none of them were compelling enough to bring to life.

Jonathan thought he had a compelling idea now and worked feverishly on it throughout the day. From time to time, when he despaired of his work, he told himself that he was doing the painting for me—because I'd requested it—or because he was trying to work out his grief. I didn't mind, even if it wasn't true. At least he was painting again.

I couldn't see what he was doing, though. Once again, my view was blocked partly by Jonathan. Why? Who chooses these vantage points for me? Why couldn't I see it at first last night, but then saw it clearly when Ruth came into the room?

David knocked on the door and peeked in.

"Go away," Jonathan said to him.

"Mrs. Wagner brought a stew for us to eat," David said. "In fact, people from the church have been bringing food all day."

"That's nice," Jonathan said without really listening.

"Pastor Joshua is here. We're going to discuss the insurance."

"Good."

"Then maybe we'll decorate the Christmas tree."

"Uh-huh."

"Then we might set it on fire."

"Good."

"Along with the rest of the house. We'll need you for skin grafts, of course."

"Right."

"If there are any survivors."

"Sure."

"You're not listening to me," David said, then stepped fully into the room—and once again, I saw the painting more fully. The group of people that Ruth had thought was a choir was not—or, I should say, it didn't look like any choir I'd ever seen. The roughly sketched figures looked more like an odd collection of people of different ages, nationalities, and vocations. The clothes and hairstyles also gave me the impression that they represented different time periods throughout history. It reminded me of the cover to the Beatles' *Sgt. Pepper's Lonely-Hearts Club Band* album. Pastor Joshua would be pleased. He was a big Beatles fan (giving us the chance to engage in the "Beatles versus Elvis" argument repeatedly). That's as much as I got to see before Jonathan threw the cover over his work.

"I want to see it," David said, taking a step toward the canvas.

"No. Only when it's finished."

"Will I live so long?" David asked as a challenge, then left the room.

Jonathan froze in position, staring at the blank canvas cover, stung by his brother's taunt. His features stiffened. I thought he might race after David and stab him with a paintbrush. Instead, he glanced at the cardboard Elvis and asked, "Did your family ever treat you like this?"

In the living room, David was back in his element as he and Pastor Joshua finished double-checking and signing the insurance forms. Joshua looked better than he had yesterday, less tired and less grief-stricken. The "business" of being a pastor helped. He was faintly humming "In My Life" by the Beatles. He'd been listening to it repeatedly since my death, and now it had buried itself in his subconscious, recycling itself whenever he wasn't thinking about anything in particular.

I was aware that my death affected him at a deeper level, beyond the loss of a close friend. It reminded him that he was getting old and that many of his closest and dearest friends—including his wife who died two years ago—were leaving him behind. In a surprising jump in my point-of-view, I suddenly see him as an old man who has outlived them all. His faith in God will then be tested by a dark loneliness, and he will ask God again and again why he lives on past any obvious usefulness. The answer will come, but it isn't one that I can hear from my present position.

"Thank you for all you've done," David said to Joshua. He flipped over the last page of the insurance documents. Business was concluded. "I appreciate your help with all the arrangements and details."

Joshua bristled a little at the formality of David's tone. "You're welcome."

"When all of his accounts are settled, I'd like to make sure you get something for all your work. You or the church. You can decide." David shoved his gold pen into his shirt pocket.

"I don't want anything from you, David," Joshua said firmly. "I'm doing this for your father."

David picked up the tone in Joshua's voice. "Suit yourself. It wouldn't have been very much anyway. Not the way my dad handled money."

"I disagree. Your father had a good head for money."

David snorted.

"You don't believe me?" Joshua pressed.

"I've spent most of the day going over his finances," said David. "'A good head for money' is not a phrase I'd use about my father."

Joshua sat back in my easy chair and folded his arms. I knew the position. He was bracing himself for an argument. "Granted, he wasn't the success that you are—at least, not the way the world defines success."

"You can say that again," David chuckled.

"But don't you think your father was rich in a far more important way?" Joshua asked.

"What way?"

"He was rich in goodness, in people."

David leveled a cool gaze at Joshua. "I'd say that a lot of people around here were rich in my father's goodness."

"Which is how your father wanted it. 'You only take with you those things that you give away,'" Joshua said.

"I don't remember that Bible verse."

"It's not a Bible verse," Joshua explained. "It was in the movie *It's a Wonderful Life*. George Bailey had it hanging on his office wall—next to a photo of his father."

David was unimpressed. "Tell me, Pastor. What do you know about the Foster Fund?"

"The Foster Fund?" Joshua was taken aback. "Why? What about it?"

"My father gave a lot of money to it. I'd like to know more about his investment."

I was curious to see how Joshua would skate around the inquiry, knowing he wouldn't want to excite David's suspicions. "Your father was a responsible man. What difference does it make now who he gave his money to?"

David continued his poker-faced expression and tone. "It makes a lot of difference to me."

"Why?"

"Because, for years, I've tried to figure out why my father did what he did with his money—why my father did a lot of the things he did. This might help me."

Joshua was unfazed. "David, do you really think you'll understand your father better if you can sort out his bank statements—figure out where his money went? Is that what you're after?"

"Maybe. Aren't you the one who always said that where a man's treasure is, that's where his heart is, too?"

"That saying didn't start with me," Joshua chuckled. "But try to remember that while a stack of canceled checks and receipts may be an *indicator* of your father's character, they're not the final measurement. They're still only numbers and piles of paper that'll turn yellow and crumble into dust one day."

Just then the front door was thrown open and Ruth swept in, her arms burdened with groceries and clothes boxes. "Did you see the snow? It's beautiful out there," she said as she blew through to the kitchen.

Pastor Joshua rose. "I have to be going. If there's anything else you need before the funeral tomorrow, just let me know." He pulled his coat on as he moved toward the door.

David followed behind. "I'll call you later with the list of hymns for the service."

Joshua put on his gloves. "David, if you want to know your father, then you have to know the One he knew. The measure of a man isn't in a box of receipts—or even in the box we'll bury him in. The measure of a man is in here." Joshua tapped his chest. "A changed heart."

After Joshua left, David remained at the door, struggling with what Joshua had said. "Typical Baptist bumper-sticker theology," he muttered. Accompanied by the sound of Ruth banging around in the kitchen, he wandered to the undecorated Christmas tree, brooding. A photo of Elvis peered up at him from the cassette case on the end table. Ruth started to sing "Blue Christmas" in the kitchen.

"You're surprisingly chipper," David called out to her.

"I feel good for some reason," Ruth replied, coming back into the room as she removed her coat. "I dreaded going to town, but it turned out all right." She hung up her coat in the front closet. I was surprised. She'd been upset when she left Ted. What had happened in the meantime?

"It's probably just the first day in three years you haven't had a hangover."

Ruth frowned at him. *You're hateful, do you know that?* her expression said. She was determined not to let David spoil her mood, though.

David smiled. "Did you meet up with Teddy boy?"

"Yes, and we had hot chocolate at Michelle's."

"Ah. Just like old times."

"He wants me to move back," she said nonchalantly.

"Now there's a joke."

"Why?" she asked.

"Oh, come on, Ruth. You? Back in Peabody?"

Now she felt defensive. To hear her own words and attitude coming from David was annoying. "What's wrong with that?"

"You're too sophisticated for this town now."

"Is that what you call it? Sophisticated?"

"What would *you* call it?"

"I'm still trying to figure that one out." Ruth grabbed a box of ornaments next to the tree and pulled it out to the center of the floor.

"Be serious, Ruth," David said. "You've moved on to bigger and better things. You'd suffocate here."

"What makes you so sure I'm not suffocating in Pittsburgh?"

"You probably are, but that's from the pollution. I'm talking about something else."

"Like what?" She sat next to the box and stared up at him.

He looked at her as if the need to explain himself was ridiculous. "Well . . ."

"Well what?"

"It's so *backward* here."

"What do you mean by 'backward'?"

He rolled his eyes. "You know what I mean. It's . . . innocent to the point of absurdity."

"And I'm not innocent anymore?" she asked. She wanted to know what her older brother really knew about her life.

David didn't answer, but threw her a warning glance by way of a cocked eyebrow.

"When did you become so cynical?" Ruth asked, with no disguise to her irritation.

"When did you become so naive?"

She didn't answer.

David went to the sliding glass door and looked out at my backyard. "A town like Peabody might be charming on a day like today, when the snow makes it look like a cheesy imitation of a Norman Rockwell painting, but to live here indefinitely? Not a chance. What could you possibly like about it?"

"The innocence you just dismissed, for one thing," Ruth replied sharply. "They still put a nativity scene on the city hall lawn. That'd be against the law in Pittsburgh."

"Nativity scenes? Is that what you want?"

"As I walked down the street, people kept stopping me to say how sorry they were to hear about Dad. I had forgotten how ..." She searched for the right word. "I'd forgotten how *human* people can be."

"Just like a scene out of *It's a Wonderful Life*, right?" David turned to her. "George Bailey with an armload of newspapers about his brother's war medals. The town rejoices."

"Something like that."

"This isn't Bedford Falls, Ruth."

"Yes, it is," Ruth said. "And you're Mr. Potter."

"Oh, please," he said wearily. "Is that how it is? The successful older brother gets pegged as Mr. Potter? Or maybe I should be Ebenezer Scrooge."

"Either one suits me." She angrily pushed the box of ornaments toward him. "Here. Get started."

"Get started on what?"

"We have to decorate this tree before the guests arrive tomorrow."

"Guests? What guests?" he asked.

"Everyone's coming over after the funeral."

"Since when?"

"Tradition, remember? They started it in this town when great-grandma died."

"That's ridiculous!"

"Don't you remember after Mom died?"

"No ..."

"Oh, that's right," she said sarcastically. "You had to go back to New York right after the funeral. Business as usual."

David stared at her, genuinely perplexed by her attitude. "There wasn't anything here to be done."

"Except console Dad."

"Right," he scoffed. "I would've been good at that."

"You'll never know, will you?" she growled and gave him a steely look. "Anyway, it's already arranged. It's probably best that way. Grieving alone together—we'd probably kill each other in the process."

David shook his head. "I don't want a lot of strange people coming over."

"Strange people? David, a lot of these folks used to be our friends."

"No—they were *your* friends and *Dad's* friends. They weren't mine." He gave the box of ornaments a gentle kick. The balls inside rattled.

"You make me so mad when you get like this," Ruth said. "And only because of the funeral and what's left of the Christmas spirit, I'm not going to give you a black eye." She nudged the box at him and stormed out of the room.

"Wait a minute," David called after her. "I'm *not* decorating this tree. Ruth!"

She didn't answer. We heard her footsteps pound up the stairs. With his hands on his hips, David stood for a moment. His eyes moved indecisively between the empty tree and the box of ornaments. Growling, he pulled out a box of lights, which I'd carefully put away the year before. I hated tangled light cords and had wrapped this string around a large piece of cardboard. He slowly unraveled the cord and began a slow rotation around the tree to put the lights on the branches.

Suddenly he faded—or dissolved, to use the film term—and I now see a younger version of myself putting the lights on the tree. Kathryn is nearby unpacking another box of Christmas balls and my heart lurches.

Kathryn.

She looks so real, so vibrant and alive. I wish—beg— for my younger self to turn and take her in his arms. Hold her close right this minute and tell her how much he loves her, how much he can't live without her. But my younger self carries on with the task at hand.

Where is she now? I wonder with a tearful ache. *Why am I seeing this? Will we be reunited soon?*

There are no answers, and the scene continues. Kathryn is pulling out the Christmas balls. David and Jonathan as children are playfully wrapping Ruth, who is barely walking, in silver tinsel. She giggles with delight.

Even in this faraway place, I can feel the warmth and the love.

Someone knocks at the front door. The child David runs to answer it and is surprised to see a stranger standing there, hat in hand. He frowns. He knows what the man wants. With undisguised boredom, he calls for me. I go to the front door and recognize the man. J. P. Coleman. He was laid off from the coal mines the year before. He and his family have been in dire straits ever since.

Now I realize that this is David's memory I'm seeing, and not mine, for as I watch myself step outside to greet J. P.

on the porch, our point-of-view stays inside, near David. He watches as I give the man some money for food, David's expression showing deep distrust and resentment.

After J. P. leaves, I mess up David's hair as I pass by to return to the tree. He looks up at me with a frown that, at the time, I didn't see.

The home movie runs out to a white screen, then suddenly switches to another scene. The look of the family and the living room is much the same as the previous scene; we are all the same ages as before. But the room is now cluttered with unwrapped gifts, and children in their pajamas are in the throes of Christmas-morning excitement.

Kathryn and I sit on the couch, she in a new robe and I in trousers and a T-shirt adorned with a new tie. Jonathan and Ruth are over-the-moon with what they find behind the tree. Ruth gets a nice rocking horse. Jonathan discovers a beginner's paint set, complete with easel and box of paints. David tears into a large box, tearing down the sides so we can all see a small metal car—modeled after a flashy red Stingray. At first he is overjoyed and nearly kills himself climbing in. Then his expression changes as his feet hit something he didn't expect. The car has pedals. He looks up at me.

"But I wanted one with an electric motor—like the one in the catalogue!" he says.

"It was too expensive," I explain. "This one is just as nice—better exercise, too," I add as a half-joke.

David holds onto the steering wheel, jerking it back and forth angrily. "But I want the electric one!"

"David!" Kathryn rebukes him.

"I'm sorry, son. We couldn't afford it," I say.

Suddenly I see in David's mind a replay of J. P. getting money from me at the front door.

"You can't have everything you want," my younger self says, which seems to add insult to injury, unbeknownst to me.

"Yes, I can!" he shouts as he rushes from the room.

At the time, I had thought it was an incidental moment—David overreacting to his disappointment over the car and throwing a tantrum. To my mortal eyes and sensibilities, it *was* an incidental moment. But it proved to be formative in ways that much larger and more seemingly significant moments weren't.

After my father died, I found a box of his journals in the attic. He'd kept them all the way back to his childhood. They were filled with brief notations about the activities or events of the day: he'd gone to the dentist, the price of bread and milk had gone up, a heat wave one particular August. Rarely did he mention the doings of our politicians in Washington or the conflicts in Europe. His life was filled with incidentals, not history-shaking events. Yet those incidentals were often profound in their impact. A scribbled note from his teenage years said simply, "Valentine's banquet tonight at church." That was where he met my mother. Another notation on a day much later in his life: "Dr. Benson—have eyes checked." That eye exam brought the doctor's attention to some irregularities that led to the discovery of a malignant brain tumor. My father died from it. Perhaps in life there are no incidentals.

Back at the Christmas tree, the adult David stopped to look at how he'd arranged the string of lights. But his mind was not on the lights. "Was it too much to ask?" he said.

I tried with all my might to answer him, wanting to shake the tree, move a piece of furniture, do something to let him know that I was nearby, that I knew, that I understood. But whatever I may be, I am not a poltergeist. Nothing moved; he did not hear me. Instead, he pushed the play button on the cassette player and Elvis sang "If Every Day Was Like Christmas."

"More Elvis," he groaned. "Doesn't he have any Johnny Mathis around here?"

I didn't.

Seven

In the attic, Jonathan had fallen asleep fully dressed. Ruth, still angry with David, peeked in on him. She smiled at the disheveled lump on the bed, and I sensed the enormous love behind that smile, a clear indication of the bond between the two of them that neither had ever had with David. I had often blamed that on David's stubborn aloofness. But I now understand that the difference really had little to do with David: Ruth and Jonathan were kindred spirits. In spite of the five years between them, there was an unspoken empathy, a bonding of the heart that could never be pinpointed to personalities or social circumstances or upbringing. It was—dare I say it?—something mystical.

Curious about Jonathan's progress on the painting, Ruth ventured near the covered canvas. She lifted the cover as quietly as she could and saw how it was taking shape. Jonathan had finished the sketch of the crowd and had even begun adding colors. There was no doubt now that the crowd was representative of a multitude of people from different countries and walks of life. I remembered that Norman Rockwell had done a painting with a similar idea. But this was no Norman Rockwell. This was in the style of Jonathan Lee—a sparse style in which only a few lines and the simplest of colors conveyed meaning beyond the obvious. *Minimalist* is probably the closest word to use. The diverse crowd was gathered around a manger scene. There was no mistaking Mary and Joseph, the shepherds and the wise men, as they knelt next to the makeshift crib. But the baby in the crib was unfinished. The baby's arms and legs were exposed, curled upwards as newborn limbs are inclined to do, but the baby's face was merely a circle.

"Get away from that," Jonathan snapped from the bed.

Ruth jerked the cover back in place. "Why?" she asked, startled. "It's beautiful, Jonathan! It's wonderful!"

"It's not finished! I can't finish it."

"What's wrong? Why can't you?"

He closed his eyes wearily. "I tried everything I could. The baby Jesus . . . nothing would work. I couldn't paint him. I couldn't do it. I knew all along I couldn't do it."

"What are you talking about? You *can* do it. It's a baby. Just paint a baby!"

"It's not that simple. It's the baby *Jesus*."

Ruth frowned. "Jonathan—now isn't the time to be the temperamental artist. Just *do* it!"

"I tried," Jonathan said as he shook his head. "I was up most of the night trying. It's useless. For a nickel, I'd break it up for the fire."

"You won't!"

"It's terrible."

"You won't! You *can't!*" Ruth insisted. "Promise me, Jonathan. Promise you won't hurt that painting."

Jonathan brooded silently.

"I won't leave this room until you promise."

Jonathan considered for a moment, then nodded slowly.

"Finish it, Jonathan. You can. I believe in you. Just like Dad always believed in you," Ruth said. He didn't answer her. Knowing she could do no more, she moved toward the door. "I have your word," she said.

Jonathan nodded again and Ruth left. Looking up at the ceiling, Jonathan sighed deeply.

Ruth wandered like a ghost through the house. She felt badly for Jonathan in the attic and was annoyed with David in the living room. Where was she to go? She considered reading in her room, but the décor—unchanged since she'd left—was too much of a reminder of her past life. She browsed through several novels in the hallway bookcase and on the shelves in my room. Nothing appealed to her. I suspected that she was really looking for something about her mother or me, a photo she hadn't seen before, a diary or journal that might give her a revelation about our past.

I thought of my own father's journals again. When I'd found them in the attic, I'd naturally looked for the day I was born to see if he'd written anything to mark the occasion. He had. "Baby boy born at 10:30. Red and wrinkled. I'm so proud." That was all, but it meant more to me than if he'd written an entire book about how much he loved me.

Now, as Ruth poked around, I wished I had kept journals for her to find.

She decided on a book by Frederick Buechner that I hadn't had a chance to read, then went into the bathroom to have a hot bath. Unlike modern tubs that are really only useful as shower stalls, our tub was an old-fashioned, claw-footed monster that a person could easily stretch out in. Kathryn used to say that the tension simply dissolved away in that tub. Ruth followed her mother's lead.

I returned—or was returned—to the living room, where David had given up on the tree and opted to pace around the room. He was still agitated from his memories of Christmases past. The Elvis tape played in the background, though David insisted on humming Johnny Mathis's "Winter Wonderland" with a vengeance. The juxtaposition of the two singers and their incompatible styles was hardly bearable. I was rescued by a knock at the door.

David was certain it was another casserole, soufflé, or pot of stew from some well-meaning member of my church. He scowled, crossed the room, and opened the door with an artificial smile in place. Ted Hagan stood there, carrying a sled. He was dusted with snow as if he'd fallen off the sled once too often. His cheeks were a ruddy red and his eyes were wide, watery, and filled with life.

"Hi, David," Ted said sheepishly. "Is Ruth here?"

"Uh-huh," David replied, scanning Ted from head to foot.

"I've been sledding with Dale Johnson and his kids," Ted explained as he tried to knock the snow off his coat, trousers, and boots.

David gestured. "Come in."

Ted started through the door.

"You might want to leave the sled outside."

"Oh," Ted said, embarrassed, and put the sled on the porch. Inside, he sat down on the couch while David called up the stairs for Ruth.

"She'll be right down," David said without knowing for sure that it was true.

Ted nodded. "Thanks."

David didn't bother with social amenities like casual conversation. He continued to pace.

After a moment, Ted asked if there was anything hot to drink.

"Like what?" David asked.

Ted eyed him for a moment, then said, "I'll find something, if you don't mind."

David shrugged.

Ted had finished making himself some hot chocolate and had walked back into the living room when Ruth came down the stairs in a bathrobe and my wife's oversized pink slippers, her hair up in a towel. She said, "Did you call me just—" and then she saw Ted. She shrieked.

"Hiya," he said.

"What are you doing here?" she asked as she turned crimson, then glared at her brother. "Why didn't you say we had a guest?"

"It's only Ted," David said without looking up.

She puffed at David, then excused herself. "I'll get dressed and come back down."

Five minutes later she returned, her hair still wet, but the bathrobe and slippers traded for jeans, flannel shirt, and thick hiking socks. In the meantime, David had slipped into his overcoat and announced that he was going out for awhile. He was gone before Ruth could ask where he was going.

Alone with Ted now, Ruth asked, "So what *are* you doing here?"

Ted went over to his coat and produced a green scarf from an inside pocket. "I think you left this at Michelle's. I'm returning it to you."

Ruth glanced at the scarf. "It's not mine."

"It isn't?" Ted asked. Undaunted, he thrust the scarf into her hands. "Well, then, Merry Christmas."

"What?"

"It's a gift," he said. He walked over to the Christmas tree.

"But—" She noticed the price tag still on the scarf.

"I needed an excuse to come over," he smiled.

Ruth giggled. It was a sound I hadn't heard from her in a long time.

"You haven't gotten very far with this tree," he said.

Ruth wrapped the scarf around her neck and joined him in front of the neglected Scotch pine. "No. I left David to do it, but he wasn't interested."

"He didn't look very happy. Is everything all right?"

"I think my family is headed for a nervous breakdown," Ruth said.

"What?"

"You know: cracking up, going nuts, crazy as a bedbug, mad as a March hare . . ."

"Really?" Ted asked as he picked up a gold ball and hooked it to a limb on the tree.

Ruth grabbed another ornament and also hung it up. "Why can't we mourn like other families? Why can't we just sit around and hug each other and cry like normal people? I've got a depressed artist upstairs who can't finish a painting—and an obsessed brother who can't balance my dad's checkbook—and I—" She was suddenly aware that he was looking at her. "I have to finish this tree."

"Finish what you were going to say," Ted said gently. When she didn't speak, he prodded her. "What's happening to *you*, Ruth?"

"Nothing."

"I'm sorry that we argued at Michelle's," Ted said. "It was rude to be so opinionated."

"Forget it," she replied. "It was silly to argue."

Ted fiddled with a few more ornaments. "I have a confession to make. I saw you after you left Michelle's—"

Ruth glanced at him suspiciously.

He said quickly, "It's a small town and I decided to take the afternoon off. You were walking down the street with a bunch of shopping bags in your arms. Your cheeks were all red from the cold, and everybody was talking to you."

"You were following me?"

"No. I was *looking* for you. But when I found you, I realized it'd be better not to bother you. I didn't want to spoil your day by making you mad at me twice."

Ruth gazed at Ted silently.

"You didn't look tired," Ted said as if that was his whole point. "You looked healthy and good. Admit it, Ruth. It felt good to be back."

"I felt good," she said. "It was a brisk, invigorating day."

"You like being back."

"It has its moments."

"What would it take to . . ."—He shuffled nervously—"to get you to come back home, Ruth?"

Ruth turned her attention to the tree again. "I don't want to talk about this, Ted."

"Why not? It's a simple question."

"I told you."

"Sorry. I don't buy this big-city/small-town stuff. There's something else. What is it?"

Ruth shrugged like a small child.

"I know you're a very proud woman and—"

Ruth looked at him. "Proud?"

"You're afraid of what people will think," he clarified.

"Why should I care what they think?"

Ted smiled at her. "Why *do* you care what they think?"

"I don't," she said without conviction.

"You do. I know you do. Maybe you can fool some of the folks around here, but you can't fool me. I know you too well."

"What makes you think I care?" She turned away from him and went to my small stereo tucked into the bookcase. She pretended to look for something to play—Elvis had finished.

Ted watched her for a moment. "I love you, Ruth. I never stopped loving you."

Ruth settled for an old Firestone Christmas album with singers such as Julie Andrews, Robert Goulet, and the

Mormon Tabernacle Choir. She hit the play button. "Silent Night" began.

Ted continued. "This isn't just a small-town boy with a crush. I know what love is. And I love you."

"You don't know what you're saying, Ted," Ruth said without looking at him. "You don't love me. You don't even know me. You knew the old Ruth, the Ruth I used to be, the Sunday-school-small-town-cheerleader-simple-and-true Ruth. I've changed. I've been through some things . . . done some things . . ."

"Old Ruth, new Ruth, I don't care," Ted affirmed from his place next to the tree. "I love *you*—whoever you were, whoever you are."

"You can't. Nobody loves like that."

"You're wrong and you know it." Ted held a small wooden train engine in his hands like a wise man offering a box of myrrh to the Christ child. "There is a love like that. What do you think Christmas is all about?"

She didn't answer.

"Maybe we can't love the way *he* loves, but we can do our best." Ted took a step toward her.

"You don't understand," Ruth began, and stopped.

Ted pressed on. "I know what the problem is. You think you've been a terrible person. You think you've done things that nobody in this small town could possibly understand, especially not me or your dad. Maybe you have; maybe we can't understand. But *I* understand that I love you, no matter what you've done." He moved so that she was looking right into his eyes. "Now what are you going to do about it?"

"I don't know," she whispered and sat down on the couch. "I don't know what I want."

Ted sat down next to her. He nervously took her hand in his. "I know one thing you want. The same thing the rest of us want. A clean slate. A sense of *forgiveness*. Well, you were raised a Christian and you know where to find forgiveness. You remember."

Ruth nodded. She swallowed back the tears. But they came anyway.

Eight

Carmichael's was a ramshackle building with no windows, loose siding, a wide front door with a tacky diamond design on the front, and a half-lit sign that said *C rm cha l's*. It had started off forty years ago as a tavern that later proclaimed itself a bar, then a sophisticated lounge, then a pub, then a sports bar (after Billy Carmichael replaced the nineteen-inch TV above the bar with a thirty-five incher), and was now considered merely a dump by most of us who lived within walking distance of it. It wasn't really a bad place—though, as a Baptist, I never could have admitted such a thing. Kathryn and I had gone inside a couple of times because Billy Carmichael had an even more extensive collection of Elvis paraphernalia than we did. He'd won an award from the National Elvis Fan Club for building a duplicate of Graceland out of sugar cubes. Got on the network news, too.

David sat at the far end of the horseshoe-shaped bar, next to the cheaply paneled wall, under the gaze of a buxom blonde on a large poster advertising a beer. From the way he hunched familiarly over the bar, an observer might have thought it had been his favorite haunt for years—except for the odd looks he kept getting from the other patrons. In his expensive Mack and finely tailored clothes, he stuck out among the plaid hunting jackets and worn coats like the sore thumb he was. He was drinking what I thought was a Coke, but then I noticed when he asked for another refill that it was Jack Daniels.

"That's the last one," Mickey, the bartender, said. He scowled openly at David.

"I can have as many as I want," David insisted, his voice thick from too many drinks. "It's a free country."

"Nothing's free in this bar." Someone laughed nearby. I think it was Walter Irving, owner of Irving's Towing Service.

"That's your last drink," Mickey said firmly.

David reached into his pocket and pulled out a wad of bills. He slapped a twenty onto the bar. "There."

Mickey took the twenty, then said, "That's still your last drink. I'll use this to call you a cab."

David frowned. "What's your problem anyway?" It sounded more like "Whatsyurprobumanyway?"

"Your father's funeral is tomorrow, isn't it?"

"Yeah—so what?"

"So I think it's disgusting that the son of Richard Lee would act like such an ass," Mickey said. Mickey was always a good kid. I taught him in Sunday school when he was in eighth grade.

A large, heavyset man I didn't recognize slid—if *slid* is the right word for the movement—over a couple of stools and took a good look at David. "You're Richard Lee's boy?" he asked with a worse slur than David's.

"Yeah."

The man clapped him on the back just as David was about to drink. Half the contents of the glass went down the front of his clothes. "Hey!"

"I liked your father," the man said, his jowls shaking merrily. "He was a good man. Gave me a job when I needed one. I cleaned his office."

Now I recognized him. It was Oz Trent. He'd put on a lot of weight since I'd last seen him.

"Good for you," David said.

"He was a good man."

"Yeah, yeah, he was a good man," David nodded, unconvinced.

Oz took a closer look at David. "You're the oldest, right? Donald."

"David."

"That's what I said. You're the one who did so well making money, right? Or are you the house-painter?"

"Look, I'd really like to be alone—"

"You must be the whiz-kid with the money." Oz tugged at David's coat as if to confirm it, then shook his head sadly. "Your father was some kind of proud of you kids. You and the house-painter and—you had a sister, right? He talked about you all the time." Since I hadn't seen Oz in several years, I couldn't imagine how he knew I talked about my children. Then again, maybe I talked about them more than I realized.

David looked at Oz, mildly surprised.

Oz drew his mug of beer to his lips. "He had a picture of you in his office—the one I cleaned—you on a horse. Did you ever own a horse?"

"No!"

"You were on something. I don't remember. But I cleaned that picture when I cleaned the office. You were a cute kid." Then he remembered. "You were on a bike."

David brooded as he remembered the bike. I'd bought it secondhand. It hadn't met his expectations any more than the car with the pedals had.

"What the heck are you doing in this place? You don't belong in here," Oz finally said after a long pause. "What would your father say if he caught you in here?"

"It's not likely he's going to catch me anywhere now, is it?" David said.

Carter Smith put his glass down on the other side of the bar. "Okay, that's it. I think we need to have a chat."

Carter used to be a deacon at our church until his real-estate business took off four or five years ago. Teledial, a long-distance phone company, had moved their facilities and seven hundred employees to Peabody. Carter said he needed Sundays to sell houses to maximize on the "boom." His fortunes rose and he became our local success story—the biggest since Alfred Peabody first found coal in 1922. Carter and his family lived the high life. But fortune can be fickle, and a year ago Teledial was bought out by a competitor who promptly closed them down. Suddenly Peabody wasn't the "location, location, location" that Carter so urgently needed it to be. His heavy investment in the Quail Run development behind my house didn't pay off. They had hoped for well-to-do, upwardly mobile buyers to pay exorbitant prices for their cardboard boxes. Instead, the upwardly mobile went to Brownsville and the houses at Quail Run were sold at rock-bottom prices to people who used to live in the trailer parks. Last I'd heard, Carter's business was on the verge of bankruptcy, and he'd been drinking more than he'd been working. It seems to me that Alfred Peabody came to the same end.

David squinted at Carter. "What did you say?"

Carter, a large barrel-chested man, pushed off of his stool and spoke as he rounded the bar toward my son. "I said, I think we need to have a chat."

"What kind of bar is this?" David asked Mickey. "I just wanted a quiet drink."

"*Several* quiet drinks," Mickey observed.

"I've been sitting over there for the past hour trying to figure you out," Carter said.

"Nothing interesting on the TV?" David asked.

"I've got a satellite dish," Mickey said.

"Where does it come from?" Carter asked.

"What?"

"I got it from the appliance store," Mickey explained.

"Be quiet, Mickey," Carter said, then turned fully to David. "Your sarcasm. Where does it come from?"

"My sarcasm?"

"Are you going to answer all my questions with questions?"

"I don't know—am I?"

"You're Richard's boy and yet you come in here with an attitude. You make snide remarks about us, about him—and I don't get it. What's your problem?"

"I don't have a problem." David hung his head over his drink. "He's *my* father and I can say whatever I want about him."

"Not in here you can't. Your father deserves *respect*. He was a—"

"Good man," David finished the sentence. "I know."

Carter poked a hard finger into David's shoulder. "Don't toy with me, son."

David spread his arms as if to say, "I'm not toying with you."

Carter eyed David's coat and his clothes. A light suddenly went on in his head. "Nice suit."

"Thanks."

"Must've set you back a bundle."

"I've got connections. I only pay a few dollars over cost."

Carter grunted. "You're pretty proud of that, aren't you?"

"What?"

"Getting good deals, being shrewd with your money."

"I don't like to *waste* it, if that's what you mean."

"I get it." Carter smiled as he leaned on the bar.

"Get what?" David looked confused. "Are you talking to me or did someone else come in on this conversation?"

"It's as clear as the nose on your face," Carter said.

David nearly reached up to touch his nose. "What is?"

Carter leaned forward and whispered in a thick, alcohol-saturated voice, "Look, kid, we're not so different. I know what's going on."

David whispered back, "Really? What do you think is going on?"

"You think that just because you left town and made a lot of money, you're better than people like us, people like your father."

"Is that what I think?"

"You betcha. Well, let me tell you something." He looked around as if making sure that no one was eavesdropping. Everyone was, but he continued anyway. "In my best year, I spent more on tips than you'll make in a decade. You hear me?"

"You don't know how much I make."

"I know all about raking in the cash. I've been there. I know."

"Good for you."

"And I also know a thing or two about respecting people. But let me tell you something."

David waited.

Carter leaned closer. "Making money and respecting people don't always go hand-in-hand. Are you with me?"

David blinked a couple of times. "No."

"I'm saying that just because you're rolling in the dough doesn't mean you're the cat's meow."

David looked at him, perplexed.

Carter poked him in the shoulder again, his voice rose. "What you've got in your wallet is nothing compared to what you've got inside. That's what I'm saying. It's who you are in *here*"—he poked at David's chest—"that counts. And your daddy had a lot in there."

"Here, here!" Jason Finch said, raising a glass. "He bailed me out when the bank tried to evict me a couple of years ago!"

"*More* money he gave away," David muttered.

"He gave it away and he helped people and he never seemed to think of himself. Isn't that right?" Carter asked whoever happened to be listening.

"That's right!" a few shouted in reply.

"What did you say?" Carter called out.

The rest of the bar yelled loudly, "That's right!"

I remembered when Carter filled in to preach for Pastor Bennett on Sunday mornings when Joshua was away. He spoke in the great Baptist tradition of tent revivals and Bible-thumping and had our old church rocking with "Amen!" and "Praise the Lord!" If he'd kept on, the gang at Carmichael's might have responded to an altar call.

David looked at Carter expectantly. But Carter had run out of steam. He poked David in the shoulder one last time and said, "I think it's time to go home." He staggered away.

None of this helped David's mood. He struggled off his barstool, endured a vigorous farewell handshake from Oz, and made his way to the door.

Mickey was on the phone. "I've got a cab coming for you."

"I'm walking home," David announced. "You can keep that twenty. Consider it another *donation* from my family."

That was supposed to be a final rebuke and a strong exit line, except that David marched into the ladies' room instead of marching out the front door as he'd planned. The patrons of Carmichael's applauded when he emerged, redfaced. He stumbled out the correct door.

"I'm almost positive he was adopted," Oz said and drained the last of his beer.

I watched David stumble home, and his drunken state told me two things. One: he obviously didn't drink very often. Two: he should drink even less, because he made a silly-looking drunk. The alcohol had loosened him up considerably. He sang "Rudolph the Red-Nosed Reindeer" loudly and in a minor key. Old Mrs. Fitzgerald turned on her porch light and threatened to call the police. David threatened to have her committed. The frozen snow crunched under the soles of his shoes. He liked the sound: when he was a boy he had told me that it reminded him of eating a bowl of Cap'n Crunch.

He tripped going up the three steps to the front porch and collided with the front door. After a minute or two of negotiation, he got it open and walked into the darkened living room. The only light came from the Christmas tree, which Ruth and Ted had decorated. The lights, tinsel, and ornaments sparkled and shone like a soft-focus picture from *Better Homes and Gardens*. Attracted by the glow, David stumbled over to the tree and stared at it. There was no guessing what his blurry eyes saw there. Slowly he got down on his knees, like a child ready to open a Christmas present, and stared at the flashing bulbs. "It's beautiful," he whispered, with an awe I hadn't heard from him for years.

Jonathan walked in from the kitchen carrying a glass of milk. He was wearing my old robe. "What in the world ... ?" He turned on a light.

David spun around and shrieked as if he'd seen a ghost.

Jonathan nearly dropped his glass of milk. "David!"

David pointed accusingly. "You're wearing Dad's robe! How dare you wear his robe?"

"I forgot mine."

"You can't wear that robe! It was a gift from me. It's . . . it's a sacrilege!"

"Only if he was the pope," Jonathan said, then walked closer to his brother. He sniffed the air. "You've been drinking."

"No, I haven't," David said. "I've been drinking."

"Of course. My mistake. Any particular reason?"

"Because it's Christmas. The reason for the season!" He giggled, then added earnestly, "I read that on a button somewhere."

Jonathan cocked an eyebrow. "Uh-huh."

"What are you doing up? Why aren't you working on your painting? Did you finish it?"

"Nope," Jonathan replied. "And it probably won't be finished either." He sipped his milk casually.

David clumsily pulled himself to his feet. "Figures," he said.

"Don't start," Jonathan said.

"I knew you wouldn't finish it. Just like you couldn't finish anything you ever started."

"I'm warning you," Jonathan said.

"That's why they threw you out of art school in New York. You couldn't finish anything. You never could."

Jonathan glared at his brother, then headed for the staircase. "I'm going to bed."

"Oh, no, you don't. You haven't told me what I want to know."

"Like what?" Jonathan asked indifferently.

"You haven't told me about the Foster Fund."

"The *Foster*—?" Jonathan frowned. "Are you back on that again?"

"I never left it."

"I told you, I never heard of the thing."

"Why should I believe you?"

Jonathan shook his head. "I'm not going to talk to you when you're drunk."

"You better, 'cause I probably won't talk to you when I'm sober." David put on what he thought was a threatening expression. It looked more like he was breaking wind. "Now spill the beans."

Jonathan folded his arms. "Why are you so obsessed about it?"

David swayed where he stood, his face furrowed into deep concentration. "Because ... because ... it's of the devil."

"Goodnight, Gracie," Jonathan said and turned away again.

David reached out for him. "Aren't you the least bit curious? Just a tiny bit?"

"No."

"Our father, who couldn't even afford to put us through school, gave his money away to that stupid fund. Money we should have had. Doesn't that bug you? Because it sure bugs me. Just like that stupid little car bugs me about everything that bugs me about me."

Jonathan leaned forward as if he'd misheard David. "What did you say?"

David dropped down on the couch and rubbed his face with his hands. "This doesn't make sense to me. I was happy with my life until now. Anybody who knows me would tell you so. I have everything that Dad *didn't* have. Do you know what he died with? He died with this lousy house in this lousy town and a lousy life insurance policy that no self-respecting dead person would admit to having. I won't die like that."

Jonathan put his glass of milk down on the end table and said, "Stand up a minute."

"Huh?"

"Stand up."

With great effort, David stood up. The two brothers faced each other for a moment.

"Thanks," Jonathan said, then punched David in the jaw. It wasn't a hard punch. Not enough to do any real damage. But David spun and fell as if he'd been clobbered by a world-class heavyweight. Jonathan stood over him and said through clenched teeth, "Don't ever talk about Dad like that. Don't ever talk like you can reduce him to little dollar signs and portfolios and decimal points in your calculator. Do you understand? You may think you're a success, but you'll never be the man that Dad was. No matter what you say or how much money you make, you'll never be the man he was."

Jonathan picked up his glass of milk and walked up the stairs.

David lay sprawled on the floor, rubbing his jaw. "Yeah, I know," he said.

Nine

From where I sit—or stand, or whatever my bodiless position might be—I am embarrassed and humbled by the comments made about me by the folks at Carmichael's. Jonathan's loyalty touches me deeply, as well. But I do not see myself now as they remember me. As I've said, I feel a sense of peace and clarity of mind and emotion in my current state. This does not mean I am stoic or emotionless. I'm feeling emotions in ways I never felt them when I was alive. I won't try to account for death making me feel more alive. But I am not duped by the kindness of everyone's comments. I know that I was not always as selfless as I seemed or should have been. Sometimes I helped as a matter of generosity, sometimes as a matter of duty, often as a matter of instinct. My motives were not always pure. Then again, I never thought that they had to be. It was enough to take action, to do something, to do anything. Somewhere along the way I came to believe that helping others was simply the Christian thing to do.

Helping others—trying to be a good man and a decent father—was never meant to drive a wedge between my children and me. Just the opposite: I thought I was being a good example to them. But now, on the morning of my funeral, I see my three children struggling with their feelings about me.

David stood at the mirror in his room, tying and retying his Italian silk tie. His mind wasn't on it. He was hungover. His head throbbed, and his jaw was bruised and tender for a reason he couldn't remember. Had Carter hit him in the jaw? No—Jonathan had. He remembered it more clearly. Jonathan had slugged him after he came back from Carmichael's. Why had he gone there in the first place?

It hadn't been a wasted experience, he reluctantly conceded. His encounter with the regulars at Carmichael's had given him something to think about. Now, in a more sober frame of mind, he thought of Oz's comments and the picture of his younger self on the bike. Kathryn and I had given him that bike for his twelfth birthday, and by that time his attitude—aroused by the Christmas pedal-car incident—was entrenched. He'd hated the bike because I'd bought it second-hand at a garage sale. But seeds of doubt now fell into the soggy soil of his hungover mind.

Maybe he was wrong.

He thought of Carter. Not so much Carter's words, which hadn't made much sense, but what he knew about Carter's life. Carter had been a financial success and now sat drinking himself into oblivion in a dive like Carmichael's. And wasn't that exactly what David had wanted to do last night? Was he a younger version of Carter? Or, worse, was Carter a glimpse into his own future—a sort of Ghost of Christmas Yet-To-Come—if he didn't shed his obsession about all he'd been denied?

David adjusted his tie. I prayed that he would continue his line of thought. He was onto something important, maybe life-changing. But his defenses were strong. He thought again of the Foster Fund. If the car with pedals had been a symbol of materialistic denial, the Foster Fund had become a symbol of materialistic neglect. I had robbed from him to give to others—and he was going to get to the bottom of it. Why? I didn't know. It wasn't as if he could get the money back. But he seemed convinced that the answer about the Foster Fund would give him an important piece to the puzzle he considered my life to be. I hoped he was right.

In the attic, Jonathan stood fully dressed before his half-finished painting. The concept was in place: people from all walks of life, all nations, surround the Nativity in adoration. The sketches of all the people, Mary and Joseph, the shepherds and wise men, were rendered and partially painted. I was no artist, but what he'd done so far looked glorious to me. The only problem, the obstacle, was that the face of the Christ child was unfinished. Jonathan hadn't even tried to draw it. In my pragmatism, I suspected impatiently that Jonathan could have put the Gerber baby's face in there and it wouldn't have mattered to anyone. But it mattered to him.

He didn't want just any face for the baby. He wanted a face that came from his own imagination, his own heart. He couldn't see it. Shoving his hands into his suit-coat pockets, he paced angrily. "Why can't I do it? Why can't I finish that child?" he asked in lamentation.

He dropped the cover over the painting and, in a decisive move, took the canvas off the easel and placed it with finality against the wall with his other abandoned works.

Ruth nervously tidied up the living room, alternately crying for me and singing "I'll Be Home For Christmas," that melancholy World War II wish. It took on an entirely different meaning for her now. Eventually she collapsed onto my easy chair and thought, *This is a heck of a way to spend Christmas Eve.*

Christmas Eve? I had forgotten what day it was. Never in my wildest dreams would I have thought I'd be buried on Christmas Eve—or any other major holiday, for that matter. But then, why should I? Who ever tries to imagine when their funeral will take place? Still, if I'd had a choice, mine wouldn't have been during the Christmas season.

I have no doubt that it was David and Joshua who decided to have the funeral today rather than wait until, say, the day after Christmas. David's motive was probably to get the funeral over with as soon as possible so he could quickly escape from the town (waiting another couple of days would have been maddening for him). Joshua's motive was likely more innocent, arising from his deep belief that death is not the end of life, but the beginning of it, a passageway to Christ himself. Thus, Christmas Eve—a time of celebrating the birth of Jesus—would be the best time to have a funeral.

That gave me hope that, under Joshua's leadership, my funeral wouldn't be a solemn and boring affair, but a celebration of sorts.

It turned out to be both. The full choir sang, under the direction of the ever-reliable Horace Hecht, many of my favorite hymns, selected by David, Jonathan, and Ruth. Fortunately my taste in hymns spoke of life, rather than death. I enjoyed hymns gleaned from the black gospel tradition, filled with exuberance and devotion. Interspersed with the songs were short comments by people I'd known, worked with, and cared about. Joshua chose well, for the most part. Harry Reeves, a deacon I'd served with at the church, told some amusing stories about our meetings—climaxing with the one where I'd fallen asleep during one presentation and knocked the overhead projector off the desk.

Joel Lewis remembered the time I was an usher and had been asked by the pastor to put extra batteries in my pocket for the wireless microphone. Unfortunately, I put the batteries in the same pocket as my loose change—and my trousers caught fire.

Kevin Ladd told comical stories about my brief stint as coach of the young people's softball team. During one practice, I'd stood too close to the batter and got hit in the family jewels by his backswing.

Margaret Simpson recalled the first and only time Kathryn and I tried to play golf—and I was struck by lightning for the attempt. I laughed at the memory of my singed hair and eyebrows, the explosive way my belt buckle had shot off and my trousers dropped. I was left with a permanent scar around my wedding ring. I never treated lightning storms the same way again.

Our new mayor, Jeff Kennedy, had a word or two to say about my philanthropic efforts in our town. Then Ruth stood up as the representative of the family, said a few words of thanks, then wept with such heavy sobs that

Jonathan had to escort her back to their pew. Joshua recovered the moment by talking about my love of family and of the people in the town and of life in general. He reminisced about our arguments over the rise and fall of Elvis and who was better, the Beatles or the Elvis.

All in all, I was pleased. Nothing was said that didn't sound sincere or was gratuitously flattering. It felt as it was: a group of people remembering an old friend. I didn't mind that at all.

The only solemn and boring period came when Nancy Daugherty, a woman who deluded herself about her ability as a poet (and I'd made the mistake of publishing a volume of her works) stood up as a "celebrity author" (Joshua's misguided words, not mine) and read a tribute to me that she'd written the night before. The first one-eighth of it was a good effort, if one enjoyed hackneyed rhymes and a Victorian sense of mortality, with its glorification of death and propensity for cherubs and sentimentalism. A few older ladies in the congregation were moved and wept openly. It would have been all right if she'd stopped there. But Nancy had the habit of writing poems of epic proportions with what I called "trick stanzas"—stanzas that sounded as if the poem was about to mercifully end, and then it didn't. Nancy's poetry was like singing a round of "Row, Row, Row Your Boat"— you never knew if and when it would end.

It eventually did and she sat down, smiling modestly to no applause, touching lightly her loose strands of metallic hair and checking her lace collar.

After another hymn and announcement about the get-together at my house after the interment, Joshua stood and looked contentedly at the congregation. He read from Hebrews chapter 11 and said there were two things that he was sure I'd tell everyone there if I could speak from the grave. (I couldn't wait to hear this.) The first was that life is fleeting, and death comes upon us unexpectedly. Second, we must be spiritually prepared for the day when we shuffle off our mortal coils. He spoke, then, of living lives of faith through Jesus, who was and is the Resurrection and the Life. It was a rousing pulpit-pounding sermon and, apart from one or two expositional points I would've argued, it was one of the best I'd ever heard Joshua preach.

At the cemetery, I watched the crowd huddled in the cold as the coffin descended into the rectangular grave. Even there, Joshua spoke positively: The coffin and its contents, he explained, were mere vessels—empty ones—which were devoid of the real Richard Lee. He assured them that the real Richard Lee had departed for heaven, and as he said it I felt a quiet confidence that it was indeed true.

Ruth, Jonathan, and David reached the house before the guests and were surprised to see that tables had been set up and enormous quantities of food laid out, compliments of the church's Ladies Auxiliary. Joshua had made the arrangements but had forgotten to mention it to my children.

Jonathan went upstairs to change into something more comfortable. David tugged at his tie to loosen it. Ruth pressed her hands against her black dress to get rid of some of the wrinkles.

"Are you okay?" Ruth asked David.

Looking like he needed some industrial-strength Alka-Seltzer, he stood at the sliding glass door that overlooked my backyard and the path to the pond. "Just dandy," he said.

"It was a nice funeral, wasn't it?"

"As funerals go, I think so."

"Strange, though."

David turned to her. "Strange?"

"The way Pastor handled it," she said. "He turned it into a kind of—I don't know—a celebration for Dad. I kept thinking Dad was going to stand up and take a bow. I've never seen anything like it."

David mused, "Hmm. Maybe it's because of Christmas."

"Or maybe it's because of something else," she said thoughtfully.

David looked at her quizzically.

"Something Ted reminded me about last night while we decorated the Christmas tree."

"And that was?"

"What we were raised to believe." She looked at David nervously. "I think I've always believed various things just because I was supposed to, but now . . ." She hesitated. She fiddled with the cuff of her sleeve. "I think about Mom and Dad's faith—and Ted's—and it's so *real*. It's . . ."

"Simple?"

"Innocent. True."

David didn't say anything.

She continued. "On one hand, all of my jadedness and cynicism want to dismiss it—to laugh at it."

David watched her.

"It wants to snuff that faith out because that's what cynicism does." She fiddled with her other cuff.

David kept his silence.

"But I don't want to be cynical anymore," she said and looked up at him. "I want . . . to feel the way I used to. Before I got so cynical."

David stared out at the backyard again.

"Does that make sense?" Ruth asked.

He half-smiled at her. "Nope."

But it did. I knew that he knew what she was talking about.

She looked away self-consciously and softly said, "I want to have faith again." It was like a child's wish.

Before she could say anything else, voices and banging feet on the porch announced the arrival of the party.

David sighed. "It's showtime."

Ruth touched his arm reassuringly, then went to open the door.

It looked as if everyone who'd attended the funeral service had decided they couldn't pass up the good cooking of our Ladies Auxiliary. Pastor Joshua led the pack as they all crammed into the house. There must've been at least seventy people there. Huge helpings of chicken casserole, pot roast, sliced ham, potato salad, corn on the cob, sweet peas, baked beans, Vienna sausages in tangy barbecue sauce, and homemade bread were dished out onto paper plates with plastic cutlery from the church. Ted Hagan got stuck serving drinks, but I noticed that he kept an eye on Ruth no matter where she was. The mood was upbeat; people swapped stories of things Kathryn and I had done in Peabody—some of which they'd forgotten about for years.

I found such praise to be embarrassing and wished that they would move on to other topics. Ruth and Jonathan, now dressed in more casual clothes—jeans, flannel shirts, and sweaters—were gracious to all the mourners and well wishers. David stood off to the side in his expensive suit, looking uncomfortable and slightly hungover.

Occasionally, someone remembered an embarrassing story about the kids: when Jonathan got stuck on a neighbor's roof after chasing a wild Frisbee, or when Ruth got into a brick-throwing contest with Wendy Phipps and needed seven stitches in her head. Or there was the time David went to the Walkers' house and fell down their laundry chute—a full three floors—and into a large clothes hamper in the basement.

The laughter was good—and right—and I was grateful to hear it in my house once again.

David was not amused. In fact, he wasn't amused by anything about the affair. I watched as his initial discomfort turned into irritation and then anger. He stood off to the side and seethed as my wake turned into a full-fledged party.

Horace Hecht sat down at our old Kendall piano and encouraged everyone to sing a few of my favorite Christmas songs. Horace was always a well-meaning but stiff old traditionalist, so I couldn't have been happier when he suddenly launched into his own version of Elvis doing "Blue Christmas." It was the perfect icebreaker and soon everyone was singing along (complete with those awful back-up vocals).

The final verse approached and Horace, noticing how uninvolved David had been, pointed at him and shouted, "Take it!"

David merely glared at him.

Horace nodded at him encouragingly. "Come on, David!"

David suddenly pushed through the crowd and stormed to the sliding glass door.

"David!" Ruth called out, annoyed. Horace stopped playing, the room went silent, and all eyes turned to my elder son.

David stood at the sliding glass door with his back to the room. His shoulders moved as if the tension was a living force that worked through the muscles there. He then spun around to face the crowd. "What's wrong with you people? My *father* is dead! Why don't you go home and sing your ridiculous Christmas songs there!"

This time there was no ladies' room to mistakenly exit into. He yanked the sliding glass door open and marched outside into the cold winter day.

Backing toward the door, Ruth gestured with embarrassment. "No, don't go. It's all right. He didn't mean it. Tell them, Jonathan." She followed David out the door.

Jonathan smiled sheepishly. "Don't mind my brother. He's only in need of a personality transplant." Jonathan also slipped out the back door.

Somebody said, "You know, I heard he was adopted."

"What's the matter with you?" Ruth shouted, barely keeping up with David as he strode to the pond.

"Me!" David said. "What's the matter with all of *you?* We buried our father today and you're acting like you're at an office Christmas party."

"Is that the problem?" she asked breathlessly.

He continued onward.

"That's not the problem," she said. "I think you're having a nervous breakdown."

Jonathan caught up with them both. "Nice exit. You should have studied drama instead of bean counting."

"Shut up," David said.

They were at the pond now. The dim sunlight through the overcast sky gave it the quality of a black-and-white photo. I glanced at the rock where I had slipped and felt embarrassed all over again. Heart attack or no heart attack, it still seemed like a silly way to go.

"Why are you holding it in, David?" Ruth rubbed her arms, which had gone quickly cold. Jonathan gave her his sweater.

"Don't patronize me with your pop-psychoanalysis."

"You didn't cry at the funeral; you haven't cried all week," she persisted. "Why don't you let it go?"

"Where and when I cry is *my* business," he replied and paced around the edge of the pond aimlessly.

"All right, then—it's your business. So why make a scene? Couldn't you just slip away quietly?" Jonathan asked.

"It made me angry, turning Dad's funeral into some kind of holiday."

"Don't you think that's what he would've wanted?" asked Ruth.

"I have no idea what he would've wanted," David said sharply. "Look, I just want to get this whole business over with. I want to settle the estate, sell the house, and get out of here."

There was a shocked pause, then Ruth cried out, "Sell the house!"

"That's right," David said.

"Wait a minute. It's the first I've heard anything about this." Ruth's voice shook. She turned to Jonathan. "Did you know?"

Jonathan shrugged. "He mentioned it."

"And what if I don't *want* to sell the house?" she challenged them.

David groaned. "We *have* to sell the house. I don't want to play landlord. Do either of you?"

"Can we talk about this where it isn't so cold?" Jonathan asked.

David ignored him. "Unless one of you wants to move in, it has to be sold."

"No," Ruth said firmly. "It's part of the family. I can't stand the thought of it going to strangers."

"Are *you* willing to move in?" he asked.

She frowned at him but didn't answer.

"There. You want to keep it, but you don't want the responsibility," David said as he kicked at a clump of snow. Then he muttered, "I've got to get out of here. This place is driving me crazy."

Pastor Joshua rounded the corner of the path. Merciful and smart man that he was, he carried coats for my three children. Following him was a man dressed almost as nicely as David, wearing an overcoat that spoke of good taste in clothes. He had a full head of wavy, perfectly cut, silver hair. He was the kind of man who conducted himself as if age were making him a better person, not deteriorating him.

Even his walk spoke of training and integrity. I was surprised to see him. And I knew why he'd come.

"What now?" David murmured. "Is somebody going to lead us in party games? Maybe pin-the-tail-on-the-donkey?"

"Easy to guess which part you'd play," Jonathan said under his breath.

"I brought your coats. No point in your freezing out here." Joshua handed out the coats and then gestured to the stranger. "This is Kenneth Walsh, an old friend of your father's and mine. He lives in Brownsville."

The name meant nothing to them.

Mr. Walsh smiled. "You don't know me. There's no reason you should. But I know you. Your mother and father talked about you all the time."

Again, the three of them watched him in silence.

Walsh turned his attention to David. "I'm the administrator of the Foster Fund, David."

David came alive. "Oh, really?"

Walsh nodded.

"Good. This is perfect," David said, his demeanor changing. "It's about time I got some answers."

"The Foster Fund?" Ruth asked.

"If you'd like to go back inside—or somewhere else— we can talk about it." Kenneth's deep baritone was the voice of warmth and comfort.

"This is as good a place as any," David said. He put on his gloves, like a man preparing for a fight.

"What's going on here?" Ruth asked Joshua.

Joshua inclined his head toward David and Kenneth.

David asked, "Tell me about that fund. Where did the money go? What did you use it for?"

"A lot of different things," Kenneth said calmly.

David eyed Kenneth from head to toe. His expression implied that Kenneth's nice coat, his clothes, even his immaculate haircut was paid for by my money. "What are you, some kind of televangelist?"

"David, you don't have to take that tone," Joshua interjected.

"I don't mind," Kenneth said, then answered David's question. "I'm a businessman—like you. I can show you my credentials."

David grunted skeptically. "Then tell me about this mysterious Foster Fund. Why did my dad give so much of his money to it—and for what purpose?"

"Are you sure you wouldn't rather go someplace warm?"

"I'd like to know now, if you don't mind."

Kenneth shoved his hands into his coat pocket. "You were probably just becoming a teenager when your father first approached me about the idea."

"*He* approached *you?*"

"That's right. He had received a windfall from some investments he'd made as a young man and wanted to establish a fund of sorts, something to help selected colleges help their students."

"You mean scholarships?" Jonathan asked.

"That was part of it," Kenneth replied. "But, yes, he wanted to financially help hard-working students finish their education."

David stared at Kenneth.

"I suppose he was thinking about you three," Kenneth continued. "But, as was generally the case with your father, it made him think about others in need. So he started the Foster Fund."

The meaning of it all was still lost to them. Ruth and Jonathan didn't know what to make of it, nor did they understand why David had made such a fuss. David looked out over the pond. "Is that it?"

Kenneth nodded. "That's it."

"A scholarship scheme," David said.

"That's right. A lot of young people were given a chance they might not have had otherwise. I have a list of the recipients, if you want to see them." Kenneth reached for his inside pocket and produced an envelope. "You'll recognize some of the names, I'm sure. Particularly your own."

"What?" David wasn't sure he'd heard correctly.

"Those scholarships you received from the college to finish your education were drawn from the Foster Fund," Kenneth said. He handed David the envelope.

David blinked, stunned, as if someone had hit him between the eyes with a rock. He looked down at the envelope, then back at Kenneth.

"You benefited as well, Jonathan," Kenneth added.

Jonathan took a deep breath. "I wouldn't be a bit surprised."

David tore open the envelope and scanned the two columns of names on Kenneth's official letterhead. His mouth fell open. His cheeks flushed. His name was there in the middle of the list.

After a moment of silence, Joshua cleared his throat and said, "He called it the Foster Fund because Foster was your father's brother's name."

"Brother?" Jonathan asked. "My dad didn't have a brother."

"He did at one time. A twin."

Jonathan was dumbfounded. "A *twin* brother?"

"Dad had a twin brother?" Ruth repeated.

"Didn't you know?" Joshua asked, surprised. "Your father was a twin. His brother died at birth."

Now all three of them stood there with their mouths gaping.

"Just like Elvis," Jonathan said softly.

I now thought of my brother and wondered if I would see him somewhere in this place. Until now naming the fund after him seemed like the only way to keep his memory alive. But to see him here . . . to meet the brother I never knew . . . that would be heaven.

Kenneth continued. "The Foster Fund was your father's pet project—a secret he and your mother kept because they didn't want undue credit. Our instructions were that no one should know until after he died. And even then, we were to answer only those people who specifically asked. You asked."

The truth was that I'd established the Foster Fund for David. I'd realized early on in his life that he was a self-sufficient, "I wanna do it myself" child. He had a very stubborn, self-reliant streak. Since he seemed to appreciate most those things he had earned himself, as he was growing up I gave him less—less than I gave Jonathan and Ruth to some degree. I had thought I was helping him by letting him "do it himself."

As his college years approached, I decided that it would be a good idea to let him "earn" his way through— through hard work or through a scholarship as a reward for his good grades. I was convinced that if I'd simply given college money to him, he wouldn't have respected his education—or me. I wanted him to feel a sense of accomplishment.

Not until after my death did I realize that it had put a wedge between us all these years. He had obviously interpreted my approach as some kind of abandonment. It grieved my heart.

"David," Kenneth said, as if he knew what I was thinking, "if you've been hurt by this news about the fund, then I'm sorry. But I can promise you that your father's intentions were solid. He was a generous man and a good steward of his money. Personally, I'm convinced that he wanted to help you in a way that didn't look as if he were helping you. Would you have wanted it any other way?"

"Probably not," David replied softly.

There. It was out now. The truth at last. What would my children do with it?

Kenneth addressed all three of my children. "I'm going to miss your father terribly." He turned and walked back to the house.

"I'm sorry I couldn't tell you myself, David," Joshua said. "Your father's wishes, you know."

"I know," David said, then looked out at the pond. His face was screwed up as if he wanted to cry, but refused to do it. He shook his head. "I feel like a first-class fool. A *selfish* first-class fool."

Jonathan chided him. "So you can't even travel economy as a fool. You have to be first class."

"I'm a fool either way."

"Why?" Jonathan asked. "Because Dad secretly helped you through college? Nah. You're a fool for better reasons than that." Jonathan also turned and walked away.

David watched him go, then faced Ruth. "Any potshots you'd like to take while I'm down? Go on. You may never get this chance again."

Ruth said thoughtfully, "We didn't know him, did we? Not like we thought."

"No. I guess we didn't." David turned on his heels and walked off toward the other side of the pond.

Ted Hagan appeared on the path from the house. "Anyone want some coffee?" he asked.

I couldn't leave David. We sat together on a rock on the far side of the pond where he cried alone, just as he'd cried in the hotel bathroom. He closed his eyes as if he were praying.

I had hoped to be vindicated by Kenneth Walsh's information about the Foster Fund. I was, in a way. But to what end? As I looked at my son, I tried to discern what he was thinking and feeling. This time I couldn't. Like Jonathan's shoulder getting in the way of his painting, something about David blocked my seeing, or getting impressions, of where his heart was. I supposed that he had a brand-new set of issues to deal with. What was he supposed to do with this anger he'd nurtured over the years? It wasn't going to magically disappear simply because he'd been corrected about his perceptions of me. If anything, he might feel betrayed because I'd kept such a large secret from him. Or perhaps he felt tricked. What was he going to do? Would his anger win out, or would he allow for a measure of grace?

I should have talked to him long ago. I should have explained who I thought he was and how that had affected my actions toward him. I should have said that parents don't treat their children the same; they try to adjust to their children's personalities and do what's right for them as individuals. Perhaps if I'd spoken to him man-to-man earlier on, we could have had better father-to-son conversations later. But I didn't. I didn't know how he was truly feeling. *I didn't know.* As a parent, I'd always followed the basic rules I'd learned from *my* parents: love them, discipline them, and pray for them every day.

But was that enough?

I looked at the tangled emotions of my three children and suspected that it wasn't. But I was at a loss as to what more I could have done.

What more could I have done? There are no guarantees in parenting. No set formulas. No easy steps. *What more could I have done?*

"Forgive me, son," I heard myself saying.

He couldn't hear me, I knew. His eyes were still closed. His thoughts and feelings were blocked to me. If indeed he was praying, then he wasn't talking to me anyway.

He slowly stood and walked in the opposite direction from the house.

I couldn't follow him.

Ten

The winter light faded, the guests went home, many of them to prepare for the candlelight service at the church. This would be the first one I'd missed in over twenty years. Ted stayed behind to help Ruth straighten up the house. He also persuaded Ruth to go to church with him.

"Want to go with us?" Ruth asked Jonathan, who had dropped himself into my easy chair with a glass of chilled eggnog.

"No, thanks," Jonathan said. "I think I'll just sit here and listen to Elvis all night."

"Is that the best way to celebrate the birth of Jesus?" Ted asked.

Jonathan shrugged. "When Elvis sang the gospel, he sang it with his soul. It's not exactly a church service, but it's as much as I want right now."

It sounded like a decent excuse, but I knew his mind was on the unfinished painting upstairs. And the truth was, he didn't want to be reminded of it by anyone at the service.

Ruth discreetly signaled Ted to leave them alone for a moment, then sat on the arm of my easy chair and took Jonathan's hand. "That was quite a revelation today. I mean, about the Foster Fund."

"That didn't surprise me," Jonathan said. "I was more surprised by the news that Dad had a twin brother who died."

"Just like Elvis."

"Just like Elvis." He took a sip of his eggnog.

"There's more," Ruth said.

He looked at her.

"I see that knot you get between your eyes when you're thinking hard. There's something else on your mind."

Jonathan sat quietly for a moment, then said, "I was just thinking about how little we really knew our parents. I mean, if David was so wrong about Dad, then maybe I'm wrong about some things, too."

"Like what?"

Jonathan hesitated, fixing his eyes on the lights of the tree. "I didn't become the painter that Dad wanted me to be. I failed him."

Ruth's face registered surprise. "Where did you get that idea, Jonathan? Dad loved you. He was proud of your talent."

"Was he?" Jonathan asked. "Then why can't I escape this feeling that he was disappointed in me?"

"*Disappointed*—in *you?*" Ruth glanced uneasily toward the kitchen where Ted was washing up the dishes. She lowered her voice. "If he was disappointed in anybody, it was me."

It was Jonathan's turn to be surprised. "What? Not a chance. He cherished you. You were his princess. Why would he be disappointed in you?"

Ruth took Jonathan's glass of eggnog and drank some of it. "I made some bad choices. I ... did things that he wouldn't have been proud of."

Jonathan observed her for a moment, then said quietly, "Which one of us hasn't? I don't think Dad imagined we were saints."

"But I was his *angel*." Her eyes washed over with tears, but she fought them back.

Jonathan shifted in the chair to face her. "Ruth ..."

She turned away from him. He searched for the words, but they wouldn't come. They were kindred spirits with a kindred problem, and now they seemed unable to help each other through it.

"I'm sorry to interrupt." It was Ted. He came in from the kitchen dabbing his hands with a dishtowel, his expression uneasy.

Ruth and Jonathan watched him and waited. Was he going to offer them more coffee?

He said in a nervous voice, "I made as much noise as I could with those dishes, but I still caught part of what you two were saying."

Ruth blushed as she looked away from him.

"I've spent a lot of time with your father over the past year or so. We talked about a lot of things. Sometimes we talked about you." He swallowed hard. "I think you two have it all wrong."

Jonathan looked at him skeptically. "How so?"

Ted sat down on the edge of the couch and twisted the dishtowel around his hands. "This is out of line, I know. But I hate the way you guys keep torturing yourselves. I ... I think you have to stop and ask yourselves a question."

"What question?"

"You have to ask, who's talking here?"

Ruth and Jonathan glanced at each other. "What do you mean?" Ruth asked.

"Is this your father talking—or your guilt?" The towel was wrapped tightly around Ted's left hand. His fingers turned red. "What you're saying doesn't sound like your father at all. He never talked like he was mad or disappointed with you."

"He didn't?"

"I know he hated to see you do stupid things or hurt yourselves, but he never said anything about your failing him or letting him down. I honestly don't think it ever occurred to him. He loved you and wanted you to be happy." Ted paused, as if choosing his next words carefully. "If he ever suffered any heartache on your account, it was because he knew that *you* weren't happy with some of the decisions you'd made. And he didn't know how to help you fix them. Not without being intrusive, I mean. He hated the idea of being intrusive." Ted freed his hand from the stranglehold of the dishtowel. "So we prayed for you."

Ruth squeezed Jonathan's hand.

Jonathan shook his head sadly. "Well."

"Don't drive yourselves crazy second-guessing what you don't know," Ted said as he stood up. "Paint or don't paint, Jonathan. But make your decision because of what *you* want, not because of something you imagine about your father's feelings." He reached a hand out to Ruth. "And as for you, young lady," he said in an attempt to lighten the mood, then accidentally dropped the towel and stumbled while picking it up.

Ruth watched him with an expression of helpless affection.

He smiled, red-faced, and reached out for her again. "If we don't get a move on, we're going to be late for the service."

Ruth allowed him to help her to her feet. They got their coats and were about to leave when Jonathan said, "I don't care what David says about you, Ted, I think you're all right."

Ted didn't know whether it was a compliment or not, but nodded all the same.

"Do you think David is coming back?" Ruth asked. "Nobody's heard from him for hours. Maybe he took off like he did after Mom's funeral."

"His rental car is still outside and his suitcase is in his room. He wouldn't leave them behind," Jonathan said, then added wryly, "Particularly since his suitcase is worth a couple of hundred dollars."

Ruth kissed him on the cheek and left with Ted.

Jonathan sat in the dim light of the living room. The tree, which stood where the tree always stood at Christmas, glowed from green, red, blue, and yellow lights. The tinsel and ornaments reflected the colors, creating an ethereal, almost transcendent experience. Elvis's voice pervaded the atmosphere. The room had changed so little in the past thirty years that Jonathan felt as if he could be transported back through time to any point in his memories of Christmases past. First he saw himself as a boy, receiving his first paint set. He thought of his earliest drawings of Jesus' miracles—the very things that made him want to draw in the first place.

Where did I go wrong with my painting? he wondered. What had he lost along the way?

He thought again about the day's revelations. The Foster Fund, my being the brother of a dead twin, David's reactions, his own realization that he did not know me as well as he had thought. Another explanation occurred to him—that he knew me, but had allowed artificial perceptions to distort what he knew. He considered the idea in artistic terms: one can paint a portrait of someone that is exact in its duplication of the model but nevertheless misses some intangible aspect—a person's character or personality or soul. Another artist may paint a portrait that seems inexact in its depiction of the model's physical appearance, but that captures the model's heart and soul completely.

What causes that difference? Maybe it's the ability of some artists to connect to the very soul of their subject; an intuitive understanding of the person *behind* the facade of skin, hair, facial features, and body.

Agitated, Jonathan leapt from my chair and paced around the room. He wondered if I, his father, had ever sat for a portrait, could he have painted me? Technically, yes. But could he have painted the *real* me? Considering the day's revelations, he wasn't so sure that he could have. He was no longer convinced that he knew me at all.

Jonathan paced for another minute, his mind whirling in several directions. Then he grabbed his coat and nearly raced out of the house. I don't think he knew where he was going. I thought that he might go to church. He went that direction. But he strolled past it without stopping, without responding to the sounds of "O Come, O Come Emmanuel" that echoed from inside like a chorus of angels on shepherds' hills. He strolled through downtown. It was quiet. The offices and remaining shops had now closed for the holiday. The decorations, strewn across the street from lamppost to lamppost, swayed gently, the cheap tinseled letters wishing a merry Christmas to the empty sidewalk. He pressed on past the town, turned left on Sycamore, and walked past the barren trees and iron fence of the cemetery. The large gate was closed and locked, but a small entry door to the right yielded to his push. He walked purposefully through the graveyard, weaving in and out of the white tombstones, until he reached Kathryn's and my grave. He stood there, breathless, as if we'd been waiting for him and he was late.

Kathryn Anne Lee her side of the tombstone said, *Beloved Wife and Mother*, and gave the days of her birth and death. *Richard Aaron Lee*, my side said, and the rest was unfinished. I had died too quickly and around a holiday. Tommy Edmonston at his family's masonry shop hadn't yet had a chance to inscribe the rest of the information about my death.

"Just like Elvis," Jonathan said as he looked at my name. He'd known for years that Elvis and I shared the same middle name—through no contrivance of my parents, just coincidence—so I wondered why it seemed significant to him now.

"What happened?" he asked out loud, as if to me.

I didn't know how to answer. His thoughts were like an explosion. I couldn't grab one long enough to comprehend it.

"What did I lose sight of?" he asked. "The soul of my subject? The soul of my work?"

I thought I understood what he was after, but he suddenly switched his train of thought. Oddly enough, his mind went to Elvis.

Where did he go wrong? Jonathan wondered. Elvis's roots, the essence of his art, were in the gospel music of his church. Those roots and the faith they engendered had found their voice in his singing. But he had drifted away from all of that. What happened? Did he stop hearing the music? Did he forget why he loved the music in the first place? How does an artist like Elvis get lost along the way?

Jonathan remembered reading that later in life Elvis regretted moving so far away from his gospel roots. For without the Gospel, there was no blues. Without the blues, there was no rock and roll. It was said that in the days leading up to his death, he got out of bed only to sing gospel songs at his piano. It was also said that he was reading a book called *The Face of Jesus* when he died. Were these things symptoms of something deeper stirring inside Elvis? Had he recognized too late that he had lost sight of the very thing that energized his music: his very soul?

Jonathan remembered again the feelings he'd had when drawing the miracles of Jesus. What he'd lacked in technical excellence he'd made up for by his passion for the miracles—his *faith* in them. His earliest works had been energized by that faith. But something had changed. He'd become a better artist technically, but . . .

A pale moon peeked through a clearing sky. Jonathan took a deep breath and exhaled, a cloud of his breath rising into the night. He had gone the way of Elvis without realizing it. He couldn't blame his artist's block on my disappointment in him any longer. That artistic paralysis came from a deeper and more significant place. He saw that now. Like Elvis, he had lost touch with the very source of his creativity.

Suddenly Jonathan and I again see the day Jonathan brought home some pictures he'd drawn in Sunday school, including his picture of Jesus healing a blind man. But we cannot see the face of Jesus. Again I ask him why he didn't draw it, and again Jonathan looks perplexed. He frowns. "It's because *I* can't see Jesus' face. I . . . can't see it in my head," he replies sadly. Then, like a film edit, we hear his voice-over: "Mrs. Ashley says I have to know Jesus in my heart before I can draw his face."

And my reply: "Knowing him in your heart is very important, but not just so you can draw him. Remember, a person is more than lines and shadows on canvas."

Somewhere, a church bell rang. It was the Episcopal church calling its parishioners to their ten-o'clock service.

Unaware of the snow and slush, Jonathan knelt at the foot of my grave. The church bells rang again. *Come, let us adore him*, they said to the churchgoers. *Come . . .*

What my heart doesn't know, my hands cannot paint, Jonathan concluded. It was Christmas Eve, the eve of the birth of the babe in the manger, the Christ child. *More than lines and shadows,* he heard in his heart. He must *know* Christ to put him on the canvas. There was no other way back to the source of his creativity—of all creativity. He looked up at the sky and into the face of the pale moon. His eyes were misty.

"Heal my blindness," he whispered. "I believe. Help me with my unbelief."

In the face of the pale moon, he saw the face of a child.

You saw me crying in the chapel, he heard Elvis sing.

Eleven

The image fades from my sight, as if I had lost the reception on TV.

Something tells me that my time is limited now. But I don't want to leave this place, wherever it may be. I don't want to leave my children. Not yet.

As I am whisked home again, there is no doubt now that I have not been controlling what I have been seeing, hearing, or perceiving.

Ruth sat in the living room, anxiously awaiting her brothers. She'd fixed some fresh coffee and placed some gifts under the tree. The fire she'd made in the fireplace crackled, casting an orange-yellow glow over the room, trading colors with the Christmas lights. So where was Jonathan? Where was David?

In spite of the rental-car-and-suitcase evidence to the contrary, she was convinced that David had flown the coop. She suspected that he would call the rental car company and tell them where to find their car. She could just hear him on the phone, probably tomorrow, asking if she would please ship his clothes to him in a box.

The front door banged open and she jumped up from the couch. "Jonathan?" she called out.

"Just me," David said as he walked into view. His arms were laden with wrapped Christmas packages. He carefully knelt next to the tree and dumped them alongside Ruth's gifts.

"What's this?" Ruth asked.

"What do they look like?" he asked, taking off his coat. "Santa Claus has come to town."

Ruth was dumbfounded. "Where in the world have you been?"

"Brownsville. I figured the stores would be open later there. Is there anything hot to drink?"

"Coffee—and some apple cider. You walked to Brownsville?"

"Part of the way, though I didn't realize when I started walking that that's where I was going. I took a cab. That's why I'm so late coming back. It took me nearly two hours to find a cab to bring me home. Brownsville isn't much more sophisticated than Peabody, really."

Ruth gazed at the presents and then back at David. "I don't get it. When you disappeared today, I thought for sure that you'd run off."

David was in the kitchen now. Ruth could hear him pouring coffee. He returned with a mug and for the first time she saw how red-cheeked he was. His eyes were moist and alive—a startling contrast to his usual hard, cynical look. *He could have been a small-town innocent like Ted*, she thought.

"Believe me, I wanted to run. I wanted to get back to my life and my work and put this whole nonsense behind me."

"But you didn't."

"No, I didn't," David said.

"Why not?"

David shrugged. "I left an expensive suitcase upstairs."

Ruth giggled.

David sighed. "Everything I thought I knew ... was wrong."

"You're not the only one who feels that way."

"I don't like being wrong."

"Get used to it."

He smiled gently. "You probably haven't noticed, but I'm not very good with relationships."

Ruth smiled back at him.

"They're too complicated," he said. "Give me a contract that spells everything out in clear terms. Terms I can understand."

"Is that why you ran away?"

He looked down into the blackness of his coffee. The Christmas tree lights reflected there. "There are times in any business deal when you learn to cut your losses and run. That's what I do. That's why I left so fast after Mom died."

"And now?"

He stared into his cup for a moment longer, gathering strength. "I think it's time for a change," he said simply. "I want to stay here for Christmas and get things sorted out. Maybe we can try to—"

He stopped because Ruth was hugging him.

"Watch my coffee," he said, trying to keep from spilling any. He patted her lightly on the back.

Ruth let go of him and stepped away. "What about Dad? What do you think of him now?"

David tried to sound nonchalant, but his voice took on a different tone that betrayed his sadness. "Dad did the best he could with us. I know his intentions were good when he set up the Foster Fund. What else could he do with me? I was spoiled then. I'm spoiled now."

Ruth smiled and reached out to hug him again.

He stepped back. "Don't get so mushy."

"Sorry," she said, smiling.

He continued. "Maybe things would've been different if he and I had talked, if I'd let him know how I felt, rather than burying my feelings for so long."

"I'm sure that's true for all of us."

"Anyway," he said, dismissing the conversation with a wave of his hand, "that's all I have to say. I've reached my quota on soul-baring."

"Thank you for telling me," she said with mock formality.

"You're welcome."

Did I feel released with his admission? You bet I did. But more than that, I felt proud of him. I knew well what it took for him to come to that conclusion. He put the core of his very self on the line.

"What about you?" he asked.

Ruth looked puzzled, but knew what he was asking. "I don't want you to sell the house."

"No?"

"I want to live here."

"Surprise, surprise." He took a drink of his coffee. "So you want to return to small-town living after all?"

"I want to return to *something*. Something I lost when I left here." She touched her heart. "Something in here."

"Ted?" David asked.

Ruth blushed. "Maybe."

"He's a nice kid," David said. "A lot better than anyone you'll find in Pittsburgh."

Jonathan arrived then. He threw his coat on a hook and sailed past Ruth and David toward the stairs.

"Jonathan?" Ruth called out.

"Not now," he said.

"But we have to talk," she shouted after him. "You can't go to bed now."

"I'm not going to bed," he said from the stairs. "I have to finish that painting."

Twelve

I don't see the finished painting. Nor whether Ruth and Ted get married. Nor how David copes with his change of heart. The picture, for the most part, is gone. I get only one more solid image: another Christmas Eve church service. Pastor Joshua Bennett officiates, as usual. I see my three children sitting in the pew that was our usual spot when we attended together as a family. But it is like looking at them through white heat—the image swaying and changing so that my children are adults, then teenagers, then children, then adults again. Intermittently, Kathryn and I are with them, too. Young, then middle-aged, then old, then young again. Is it a visual trick, or is time passing quickly before my eyes?

I remember something that happened shortly after I learned to use a computer. The confounded word processor glitched one day and all the files and manuscripts I had stored there suddenly appeared in rapid succession on the screen. There was no order to the lightning-fast images that came and went in front of my eyes, faster and faster until the machine overloaded and the screen went blank.

What I see now is nearly like that, although far beyond it in intensity and power—mere technology could never duplicate this experience. The scenes spin past me as if they are bound by neither time nor chronology. Yet I comprehend them fully. And it occurs to me that everything I'm seeing—as well as everything I've seen since the moment of my death—I may have seen in the blink of an eye. Time doesn't exist here. For all I know, it has been the tiniest fraction of a second since I was standing next to the pond and felt that itch in my chest.

The scenes stop and the last thing I see is a young couple sitting in a movie theater watching Elvis Presley in *Blue Hawaii*. Then it is gone. My life as I know it has finished. The future belongs to the living. I know beyond a shadow of doubt that I am in an eternal—even holy—place.

I hear a voice singing "Love Me Tender." But it is not Elvis. It is my beloved, my companion. Then she is before me, and she is at once glorious to behold and as much herself as she ever was.

"It turned out all right," I say to her as naturally as if we had actually just been sitting and watching an Elvis movie.

She smiles. In the warmth of her smile, I feel a sense of completion.

"Is that what I was supposed to see?" I ask. Because she got here ahead of me, I assume she knows.

"Supposed to see?"

"Yes. Was I supposed to learn that in spite of our best efforts as parents, things go wrong and maybe they'll go right again?"

"What makes you think you were supposed to learn anything?"

"Wasn't I?"

"Maybe it was only a small reminder of what you already knew."

"Reminder?" I'm confused.

"A small reminder, before you go on to other reminders."

"Remind me of what, though? What did I already know?"

"You said it when David was sitting on the rock."

I recall the moment. "Forgiveness?"

"Forgiveness. Understanding. Reconciliation." Her voice is a balm of compassion to me. "We didn't expect our deaths to be part of the answer to our prayers, did we?"

I nod but cannot be sure of any conclusions I might draw now. "There's so much about life that's out of our control."

She smiles again and I do not see the smile now as much as I feel its radiance. "Come on. There's someone you have to meet. He's this way."

I hesitate. "Is he miffed because I became a relaxed Baptist?"

"No," she giggles.

"Should I be afraid?"

"Why be afraid?" she asks as she takes my hand. "You've come home."

We want to hear from you. Please send your comments about this book to us in care of the address below. Thank you.

ZondervanPublishingHouse
Grand Rapids, Michigan 49530
http://www.zondervan.com